THE SILENT MURDERS

The following titles are all in the *Fonthill Complete A. G. Macdonell* Series.
The year indicates when the first edition was published.
See **www.fonthillmedia.com** for details.

Fiction

England, their England	(1933)
How Like an Angel	(1934)
Lords and Masters	(1936)
The Autobiography of a Cad	(1939)
Flight From a Lady	(1939)
Crew of the Anaconda	(1940)

Short Stories

The Spanish Pistol	(1939)

Non-Fiction

Napoleon and his Marshals	(1934)
A Visit to America	(1935)
My Scotland	(1937)

Crime and Thrillers written under the pseudonym of John Cameron

The Seven Stabs	(1929)
Body Found Stabbed	(1932)

Crime and Thrillers written under the pseudonym of Neil Gordon

The New Gun Runners	(1928)
The Factory on the Cliff	(1928)
The Professor's Poison	(1928)
The Silent Murders	(1929)
The Big Ben Alibi	(1930)
Murder in Earl's Court	(1931)
The Shakespeare Murders	(1933)

THE SILENT MURDERS

A. G. MACDONELL

Originally published under the pseudonym of
NEIL GORDON

FONTHILL

Fonthill Media Limited
Fonthill Media LLC
www.fonthillmedia.com
office@fonthillmedia.com

First published 1929
This edition published in the United Kingdom 2012

British Library Cataloguing in Publication Data:
A catalogue record for this book is available from the British Library

Copyright © in introduction, Fonthill Media 2012

ISBN 978-1-78155-022-9 (print)
ISBN 978-1-78155-151-6 (e-book)

Typeset in 11pt on 14pt Sabon.
Printed and bound in England

Contents

Introduction
to the 2012 Edition

The Silent Murders is a classic of the A. G. Macdonell crime series, first published in 1929 at the height of the genre's popularity. It is one of several crime novels written by Macdonell under the pseudonym Neil Gordon.

Archibald Gordon Macdonell — Archie — was born on 3 November 1895 in Poona, India, the younger son of William Robert Macdonell of Mortlach, a prominent merchant in Bombay, and Alice Elizabeth, daughter of John Forbes White, classical scholar and patron of the arts. It seems likely that Archie was named after Brevet-Colonel A. G. Macdonell, CB, presumably an uncle, who commanded a force that defeated Sultan Muhammed Khan at the fort of Shabkader in the Afghan campaign of 1897.

The family left India in 1896 and Archie was brought up at 'Colcot' in Enfield, Middlesex, and the Macdonell family home of 'Bridgefield', Bridge of Don, Aberdeen. He was educated at Horris Hill preparatory school near Newbury, and Winchester College, where he won a scholarship. Archie left school in 1914, and two years later, he joined the Royal Field Artillery of the 51st Highland Division as a second lieutenant. His experiences fighting on the Western Front were to have a great influence on the rest of his life.

The 51st, known by the Germans as the 'Ladies from Hell' on account of their kilts, were a renowned force, boasting engagements at Beaumont-Hamel, Arras, and Cambrai. But by the time of the 1918 Spring Offensives, the division was war-worn and under strength; it suffered heavily and Archie Macdonell was invalided back to England, diagnosed with shell shock.

After the war, Macdonell worked with the Friends' Emergency and War Victims Relief Committee, a Quaker mission, on reconstruction in eastern Poland and famine in Russia. Between 1922 and 1927 he was on the headquarters staff of the League of Nations Union, which has prominent mention in *Flight from a Lady* and *Lords and Masters*. In the meantime he stood unsuccessfully as Liberal candidate for Lincoln in the general elections of 1923 and '24. On 31 August 1926, Macdonell married Mona Sabine Mann, daughter of the artist Harrington Mann and his wife, Florence Sabine Pasley. They had one daughter, Jennifer. It wasn't a happy marriage and they divorced in 1937, Mona citing her husband's adultery.

A. G. Macdonell began his career as an author in 1927 writing detective stories, sometimes under the pseudonyms Neil Gordon or John Cameron. He was also highly regarded at this time as a pugnacious and perceptive drama critic; he frequently contributed to the *London Mercury*, a literary journal founded in 1919 by John Collings Squire, the poet, writer, and journalist, and Archie's close friend.

By 1933 Macdonell had produced nine books, but it was only with the publication in that year of *England, Their England* that he truly established his reputation as an author. A gentle, affectionate satire of eccentric English customs and society, *England, Their England* was highly praised and won the prestigious James Tait Black Award in 1933. Macdonell capitalized on this success with another satire, *How Like an Angel* (1934), which parodied the 'bright young things' and the British legal system. The military history *Napoleon and his Marshals* (1934) signalled a new direction; although Macdonell thought it poorly rewarded financially, the book was admired by military experts, and it illustrated the range of his abilities. Between 1933 and 1941, A. G. Macdonell produced eleven more books, including the superlative *Lords and Masters* (1936), which tore into 1930s upper-class hypocrisy in a gripping and prescient thriller, and *The Autobiography of a Cad* (1939), an hilarious mock-memoir of one Edward Fox-Ingleby, ruthless landowner, unscrupulous politician, and consummate scoundrel.

The Silent Murders is one of Macdonell's early ventures into the literary world, and although it enjoyed only moderate success when first published, it's fast-paced narrative and ingenious plot display the flair and imagination that would soon establish him as a celebrated writer.

In 1940 Macdonell married his second wife, Rose Paul-Schiff, a Viennese whose family was connected with the banking firm of Warburg Schiff. His health had been weak since the First World War, and he died suddenly of heart failure in his Oxford home on 16 January 1941, at the age of 45.

A tall, athletic man with a close-cropped moustache, he was remembered as a complex individual, 'delightful … but quarrelsome and choleric' by the writer Alec Waugh, who called him the Purple Scot, and by J. B. Morton, as 'a man of conviction, with a quick wit and enthusiasm and … a sense of compassion for every kind of unhappiness.'

CHAPTER I

Stuck-up Sam, Number Three — Aloysius Skinner, Number Four

Very little attention was aroused by the murder of an elderly tramp on the road between King's Langley and Berkhampstead. Tramps have few relations to mourn them and few legatees to be interested. The man was found in a ditch, crumpled up as if dead-tired or dead-drunk. He was neither. He had been stabbed between the shoulders and must have died almost at once. A square of cardboard was tied to the last surviving button of the tramp's ragged overcoat and on the square was written the word "Three." Even the faint gleam of interest aroused by this peculiarity died away as soon as it was realised that there was no proof whatever that this square of cardboard had anything to do with the murderer. Tramps are an acquisitive race and pick up an extraordinary collection of objects in the course of their travels, treasuring each one until proved absolutely and conclusively to be utterly worthless. So in this case there was no reason to suppose that the piece of cardboard was anything but an item in the tramp's miscellaneous hoard of junk.

Official interest in the case lasted longer, naturally, than public interest. The influential section of the brotherhood of tramps whose beat extends from Watford to Banbury was arrested to a man. Nothing was proved against any of them but a certain amount of information was forthcoming about the murdered vagrant. He was universally unpopular among his colleagues for the obvious reason that he was suspected of having once been a man of substance who had come down in the world. He had a sarcastic tongue and an especially mean way of cheating other tramps over the purchase and sale of acquired commodities. His petty thefts, also, gave them all a bad name on the road. He was known as Stuck-up Sam or, alternatively, the Blasted Gent, and it was freely rumoured that he could read and write.

Among his belongings were found two packs of marked cards, a wire-clipper, an assortment of instruments for turning locks and a battered

Prayer Book, on the fly-leaf of which was written in faded ink, "To my darling Sammy from his Mother on his seventh birthday. May second eighteen hundred and sixty three." Assuming, a very considerable assumption, that this was his own property, it would place his age at sixty-six, would confirm his name of Stuck-up Sam and would add support to the theory that he had seen better days.

But, although the arrested and indignant gentlemen of the road agreed in moral condemnation of the dead man, they all asseverated with vehemence that their objections to his character did not go so far as murder. A line must be drawn somewhere and that was where they drew it—a good deal short of murder. The police believed them. The doors were opened and the flood of battered and tattered humanity flowed swiftly back in the direction of the road between Watford and Banbury.

Stuck-up Sam or the Blasted Gent was buried in an anonymous grave and at once forgotten. Two months later a much more satisfactory murder from every point of view, except that of the murdered man, took place in the centre of London at about, noon, probably in front of the Bank of England. Mr Aloysius Skinner, Chairman of the Imperial Cochineal Company and Director of many of the subsidiary companies of that vast concern, was shot dead in a taxi. He was proceeding from the offices of the Imperial Cochineal Company to an interview with the General Manager of the National Bank at the head office of the latter and it was assumed, from the trend of the evidence subsequently collected by Scotland Yard, that he was shot with an air-pistol through the window of the cab while it was stationary in a traffic block. The driver of the cab was positive that the only time he had been compelled to halt was just opposite the Bank of England. He was all the more positive as he had been at the time agreeably surprised at his luck in, slipping through the traffic at the most crowded time of the day. The bullet had killed the unfortunate man instantly and it was, therefore, very unlikely that it could have been fired with such accuracy while the taxi was moving. The absence of noise, or rather the fact that no one noticed the noise of a pistol-shot, was hardly surprising. But the absence of any trace of powder-stains on the body was a strong indication that an air-pistol had been used. The official theory, then, was that someone had leant into the stationary cab and shot Mr Skinner through the heart with an air-pistol.

The public was intensely gratified. The murder of an important man, whose name is a household word, whose photograph has often appeared in the evening papers, whose fortune is reputed to be well in excess of a million pounds, naturally strikes a thrill into every heart. And the thrill is intensified when the murder is committed in a taxi, at noon, outside the Bank of England. It was no wonder that people were delighted. The inner section of the public which studies detective stories and is accustomed to the sudden and violent decease of millionaires waited with the wisdom of experience for the collapse of Imperial Cochineal, for the wild scenes in the Stock Exchange, the suicide of half-a-dozen financiers and the sympathetic panic in Wall Street. To their disappointment none of these things occurred. Imperial Cochineal was too firmly founded on cash reserves and inner reserves and hidden inner reserves to wobble even to the extent of a penny a share. The board of directors unanimously voted the Vice-Chairman into the Chair and the great company continued its way unmoved.

The simplicity of the murder made the detection of the criminal difficult. The first and obvious clue to be discovered is the clue of Motive and it was here that the police at once found an obstacle. Mr Aloysius Skinner had begun life in a humble way. That was known. But he was a very secretive man and even the closest of his few friends knew nothing of his early life. He was a bachelor and had no apparent relations. Reminiscence had never been one of his foibles. But it was clearly possible, indeed probable, that a man like Mr Skinner who had climbed so successfully from poverty to riches, from obscurity to fame, must have left behind him in the process a good many enemies. His path to the Chairmanship of Imperial Cochineal must have been strewn with jealous rivals, disgruntled and discarded friends of his youth, discharged employees, broken speculators; but he had never spoken about them. For all his acquaintances knew, his life had been a quiet and unassuming record of steady progress with no sensational interludes. His will bequeathed the whole of his fortune to charities, thus ruling out the financial motive for the crime. In fact, his life, as revealed by the enquiries, seemed to, be that most melancholy of existences, the life of an utterly lonely old man.

The police had to fall back on four possible clues, excluding the theories that the murderer was a madman or had shot the wrong man.

The first was that the murderer must have known Mr Skinner's movements precisely from minute to minute. In other words, he must have been in the service of the Cochineal Company, and had thus known, on the fatal morning, that Mr Skinner was due to visit the General Manager of the National Bank, that he would take a taxi and that he would go alone. The murderer would then have stationed himself at the most likely place for a jam in the traffic and a hold-up of the taxi. This theory fell to the ground slowly as the most searching investigation into the antecedents and movements of every member of the staff of the Company failed to reveal the slightest traces of a suspicious nature.

The second theory was that the murderer was ignorant of the exact engagements of the Chairman. It followed, therefore, that he must have shadowed the offices for days, possibly weeks, before hitting on his perfect chance. It was too monstrous a coincidence to suppose that he had entered the City of London with the intention of killing Mr Skinner, had gone as far as the Bank, had suddenly seen his enemy sitting in a stationary cab and had promptly seized the opportunity of shooting him: The next search, then, was for any loafers who had been standing round Mr Skinner's office during the previous days. As might be expected, this search proved a failure. People are too busy in the City of London in the pursuit of the elusive pound sterling to have any time for loafers. The very idea of loafing is enough to make most of them shudder, if they have any time for shuddering.

The third line of investigation was the air-pistol, if indeed an air-pistol was used. The bullet was an ordinary pistol-bullet that might have been fired from any .32 automatic. The microscope showed the faintest trace of "scoring" on it where it had touched some infinitesimally small irregularity in the barrel of the weapon, sufficient to identify the pistol if it should ever be found, but most certainly not sufficient to be of the least use in helping to find it.

The fourth clue was even more nebulous as there was no evidence to show that it had not been brought into the taxi by any of the seven fares which the taxi-driver had on that day driven previous to Mr Skinner's last journey. The clue, for what it was worth, was a piece of white cardboard on which was printed in ink the single word "Four."

CHAPTER II

Oliver Maddock, Number Five

About a month after the murder of Mr Aloysius Skinner, a cheerful party was sitting down to iced drinks under the shade of a large cedar tree in a walled garden at Enfield. It had been a glorious summer afternoon, the tennis had been excellent, the three grass courts had been playing smoothly and truly, the five dozen new tennis balls had lightened the usually irksome task of ball retrieving. Everyone was hot and thirsty. The shade was cool, the ice tinkled in the long drinks. The deck chairs were opened out at full length.

Mr Henry Maddock was entertaining. The guests were, for the most part, contemporaries and friends of his son and daughter, all tennis players of enthusiasm and distinction. Young Bill Maddock was on the way towards the first flight of players and his sister Julia only required a little more severity on the backhand to keep him company. Already their entry for the Mixed Doubles at Wimbledon had been accepted and it is not everyone who can say the same. He was twenty-four and she was twenty-two years old and they lived, thought and talked lawn tennis. It is true that they enjoyed dancing, at which they were skilful, and motoring, at which they were awe-inspiring, but first and last lawn tennis was their life. They congregated round themselves a collection of friends, apparently indistinguishable from one another, with similar tastes and similar names. The tennis courts at Greenlawns resounded day after day with shouts of "Yours Bob,"

"Mine Bill,"

"Yours Judy,"

"Out,"

"Fault,"

"Leave it," and so on.

Mr Maddock himself was a keen player and by no means a bad one. He was a tall, florid, broad-shouldered man of about fifty-five, already famous in the neighbourhood, in which he had only been settled for three years, for the violence of his temper and the alleged mystery surrounding his acquisition of wealth. Odd rumours, based on no discoverable facts, circulated about a wild life in Africa and a poverty that changed with peculiar suddenness to riches. It is true that Mr Maddock had been many years in Johannesburg. He used to speak of them himself. It was also true that an elderly man, very lame in one leg, with a sunburnt face and a pointed beard and a queer rough accent had once called at Greenlawns. He had asked the way from the butcher, and the butcher and two maids who happened to be in conversation with him had seen him enter by the front door and come out again in a few minutes clean through a window on the first floor with a great smashing of glass. The man broke an arm and a couple of ribs on hitting the gravel path and the butcher took him to hospital. The incident had been hushed up—the bearded stranger refused to make a charge or to say a word—but a distinctly unpleasant feeling remained.

There was also the dog-kicking episode which had resulted in the death of an Airedale. The vet had had to destroy it. That, again, had been hushed up as far as possible and the owner of the dog compensated with a £100 note. But, naturally, local residents talked more and more about Mr Maddock and less and less to him. Only his obviously great wealth deterred them from taking the risk of being openly rude to him. One could never be quite sure to what extent a rich man, a really rich man, could and would retaliate.

The tennis parties, therefore, were not composed of neighbours but of friends and acquaintances made in London, Oxford, Eton, St Moritz and Monte Carlo. On this occasion, however, the guest of honour was not an athlete but an elderly scholar. When Henry Maddock had run away from home at the age of fourteen he had left behind an elder brother of very different tastes and disposition. Oliver Maddock had been a studious lad and had grown into a studious man. In early life he had supported himself by teaching, by copying legal documents, by translating French novels into English (he had taught himself French in the evenings after his day's work) and by many and various occupations connected in some way or other with books, study and scholarship. At the age of fifty he inherited a small income from his father and retired to lead a happy and tranquil life in a small house in the Scottish town of St Andrews. It was his first excursion north of the Tweed and he explained his choice to the few people who cared two straws where he lived by saying that he had to live in a University town and of all University towns St Andrews seemed the quietest and most remote. To the Kingdom of Fife, then, he went with a trunk containing his clothes and seventeen packing cases containing his books. He lived in the outskirts of the town, read Greek and Latin and Hebrew and Sanscrit till all hours of the morning, and never set foot on the golf links. After twenty years of this secluded existence, his younger brother returned from outlandish parts with a large fortune and insisted on providing the scholar with enough money to buy all the books he wanted and to build an adequate library to house them. In addition, the masterful Henry uprooted the docile Oliver once a year from his hermitage and transplanted him for a month to his suburban palace at Enfield, and the truth was that Oliver enjoyed these excursions into a strange and unknown life. He blinked away cheerfully behind his ancient spectacles, he drank his brother's port with great gusto and he spent most of his time in the bookshops of the Charing Cross Road or in the salerooms. But one thing he stoutly refused to do. He would not be lured into playing tennis with his athletic nephew and niece. He enjoyed watching the play, however, and talked vaguely and disjointedly about Greek sculpture and discus-throwers and Castor and Pollux. But neither his brother nor his nephew and niece cared a farthing about Greek sculpture or discus-throwers or Castor and Pollux, so his conversation was mainly directed to himself, an arrangement which he and everyone else found very satisfactory.

At first Bill and Julia and their friends had thought him rather frightening. He was so learned and looked so old and wise. But later they found that Uncle Oliver himself was extremely frightened of them and that he was not so old as he looked and certainly not so wise. So they voted him a "harmless old boy" and a "decent old fellow" and returned to their tennis. With the unerring instinct of youth they had hit upon the three adjectives which described him exactly. He was old, decent, and very, very harmless. Several of the visitors to Greenlawns thought, but wisely refrained from saying, that by no stretch of imagination or charity could the three epithets be applied to their formidable host. Henry Maddock was of a very different stamp. His size, his bushy eyebrows and iron-grey hair, his terrifying scowl when he was displeased with anyone or anything, filled even the lightest-hearted with an unmistakable feeling of awe. He looked thirty years younger than his brother and gave the impression that if he got really angry he would be anything but harmless. But as their host and entertainer no one could be more charming, more hospitable or more friendly. Visitors could always rely at Greenlawns on new tennis balls and lots of them, perfectly rolled grass courts, hard courts for wet weather, and plenty of drinks, cool and strong, when the play was over.

On this particular evening the party was spread out in a broad semicircle of deck chairs. Mr Henry Maddock was sitting, roughly speaking, in the middle of the semicircle, his brother at one end. There were thirteen guests and Bill and Julia, making sixteen players and one spectator. The butler had just brought out a second instalment of his celebrated champagne cup and retired across the lawn to the house. Suddenly one of the young men sat up in his chair and said sharply, "I say, isn't that someone in the shrubbery over there?"

He pointed across the courts to a corner of the high brick wall which surrounded the garden. The wall itself was masked by thick rhododendron bushes, and, at intervals, laburnum and lilac trees. Bill Maddock, whose face was buried in a long glass, did not even bother to look up. He mumbled, "A dog, I expect. Or a gardener."

His father paid more attention and stared hard in the direction of the young man's finger.

"I don't think so," he said at last.

"I distinctly saw a branch move," persisted the other. "There isn't a breath of wind."

"You're seeing things, Bob," said Julia, and everyone tittered. Only Henry Maddock and the young man addressed as Bob continued to sit up and stare at the rhododendrons.

"There it is again," he said sharply and Henry Maddock answered, "You're right, by thunder. There's someone there."

As he spoke, the bushes were thrust aside and a man half-stepped out. The garden was large and the semicircle of chairs was at least fifty yards from the corner of the wall, and the partial screen of leaves effectively prevented any of the party from seeing details of the stranger's appearance.

Henry Maddock raised his voice and called out, "Who are you? What do you want?"

The man made no reply. He called again, "Hey, you. What are you doing there?" There was an answer this time, consisting of a short laugh of indescribable harshness and unpleasantness, and then the stranger called back, "I want you, Maddock, and I've come for you. You're number five on my list."

There came two muffled thuds, almost like the suppressed bark of a dog or a half-accomplished sneeze, and immediately afterwards the man backed into the shrubbery out of sight.

"After him," roared Henry Maddock, leaping to his feet and leading a flannelled charge across the grass. He was twenty-five years older than the oldest of the young men who followed him, but he reached the bushes first. They were too late. The stranger had vanished and they could hear a motor car in the lane on the other side of the high wall changing from first gear to second as it moved away.

"Nothing to be done," said Maddock curtly. "What the devil did the fellow want?" He added half under his breath with a savage scowl, "And who the devil was he?"

The girls of the party came across the lawns to meet, admiringly, the return of the gallant charge. Their host swiftly recovered his composure and geniality and met them gaily.

"The fellow's gone," he said. "Over the wall like a lamplighter and off in a car. There's no harm done."

But there was harm done. Oliver Maddock was lying in his deck chair, his head fallen on his shoulder, a placid smile on his face and two bullets in his heart.

CHAPTER III

Inspector Dewar of The Yard

Inspector Dewar had been summoned to a conference with two of the famous superintendents of Scotland Yard.

"There is no doubt about the bullets," he was saying. "Henderson has been at them with the microscope and there's no doubt at all that the same pistol killed Skinner and Maddock." With these words the inspector concluded his report and waited respectfully for the comments of his superior officers. For an appreciable period no one spoke and then Superintendent Bone, a large, heavy, comfortable man, observed, "I've seen the gunmaker's report."

"Not much to go upon there," said Superintendent Lloyd sharply. Superintendent Lloyd was rather like an aged and wizened shrimp. He had somehow evaded the regulations which prescribe the height in feet and inches necessary for admission to the police force and was shorter by seven or eight inches than any other man in Scotland Yard. In addition to this shortness of stature, his whole body and face seemed to have shrunk gradually away to an extraordinary thinness. Beside his immense colleague he looked like a prematurely aged schoolboy.

"You'll get nothing from the pistol," he added in his dry, staccato tones. "Made in Barcelona or Essen. Turned out by the thousand and sold to anyone who's got a few shillings."

"That's right," said Bone. "The pistol's no good. Antecedents, Dewar my lad, antecedents. That's what you must go for."

"Yes, sir," replied Dewar. "It seems to me that we've got to find out something in common between old Skinner and Henry Maddock."

The superintendent nodded and Lloyd remarked, "Henry Maddock's the boy to keep an eye on."

"I've come across something already," replied Dewar. "Skinner had affairs in Africa and he went out there once, just before the war. He was interested in some mines. He may have met Henry out there."

"It's a problem in geometry," said Superintendent Bone. "The lives of Skinner and Maddock must intersect somewhere. Where they intersect you'll find a third party who had a down on both of them."

"And leave Oliver Maddock out of it altogether?"

"Yes. Look at his record. Twenty-three years in a villa in St Andrews. Then before that; ten years of school teaching, two years of tutoring and so on."

"Out of the question," said Lloyd.

"Then the man who shot him couldn't have known Henry by sight," objected Dewar. "You haven't seen Henry. A great bull of a man with a nasty look in his eye. Oliver was a mild little bird. No one could mix them up."

"Yes, that's odd," murmured Bone, "but it's explainable, of course. There are lots of possible reasons." The two superintendents nodded to each other and then seemed to go off into a trance. Dewar waited. At last Lloyd cocked an eye at his somnolent colleague and said abruptly, "If Skinner was number Four and Maddock number Five, where's One, Two and Three and how many more of them are there?"

"I was going to ask you that, sir," put in Dewar. "I wanted to know what you think of the tramp."

Both superintendents were interested by this question.

"What tramp?" asked the stout one.

"The tramp who was murdered on the Banbury Road. He had a cardboard with 'Three' on it tied to his coat. Rackham was telling me about it just now. Rackham handled the case.

The thin superintendent said sharply, "Rackham's report?"

"Here, sir."

They pored over it in silence and then again dropped off into brown studies. "George," said Bone at last, "it's fishy."

"It's deucedly fishy, Bert," answered the other. "Is there a common link between the Blasted Gent and the Chairman of Imperial Cochineal? Well, there might be. They were almost the same age for one thing. But where's the link between the Gent and Maddock? On the other hand, if the tramp's out of it, why the numbers? Is that a coincidence? A confoundedly odd one." He spoke dreamily, thinking aloud. His wizened colleague took up the running.

"Dewar, has Henry Maddock been in England for long?"

"About five years."

"And away for how long?" Dewar looked at his notebook.

"He left at the age of fourteen, forty-one years ago."

"And never came back in the interval?"

"He says not."

"Hm! Johannesburg might be able to confirm that. Or again they might not." And the Superintendent turned over Inspector Rackham's report. "This tramp, I see, is known to have walked that road for the last ten or twelve years. Nothing known before that. Make a note to ask Rackham to get at these tramps again and find out if the Blasted Gent ever spoke of his travels or talked of South Africa."

"Yes, sir."

"Now, this man that Henry Maddock threw out of the window. Who was he?"

"A beggar from the Rand, Maddock says. He's very secretive about his past. With good reason too I should think from the look of him."

The stout superintendent rolled a slow eye round the ceiling and said, "Do you think Henry thinks the bullets were meant for him?"

"I'm positive of it, sir," answered Dewar. "The man's not frightened. He doesn't look as if he was easily frightened. But he's very much on his guard. Carries a gun. Fitted burglar alarms and bought a couple of Alsatian dogs. Not going about much either. But he's not giving anything away."

There was another silence and then the Superintendents rose simultaneously.

"Let us know how you get on," Bone said and, linking arms, they went out leaving Inspector Dewar with his problem.

His first move was to visit the room of his colleague, Inspector Rackham, and discuss once more the affair of the murdered tramp.

"We've got to go into the antecedents of these fellows, Rackham," he said. "The tramp, Skinner and Maddock. Somewhere or other their lives meet. When we find out where they meet we shall know where we are."

"Assuming the numbers to be part of the business," said Rackham.

"Yes," agreed Dewar. "And I think they must be."

"But where's number one and number two?"

"Ah! Now you're asking. South Africa, I should think."

"Not in this country anyway," said Rackham emphatically. "I went into that when I was on the Blasted Gent affair. There's no record in the provinces of any murders with numbers attached to them."

Dewar pondered for a moment and then said reflectively, "I feel that the key to this thing is in Africa. It somehow isn't English. It's more like, foreign gang feuds——"

"You don't need to go beyond Clerkenwell for gang feuds," put in Rackham.

"No, I know. But that's a different class of thing. You don't get Chairmen of Companies stabbing each other in the Gray's Inn Road. But you might in Africa. Suppose Skinner and Maddock and half a dozen others combined to do a dirty trick in Johannesburg on somebody else and that somebody else came out of prison recently and started to get a bit of his own back. Eh? What about that?"

"And the tramp?"

"Either one of the crowd who'd come down in the world or a spy or an informer. It's possible, you know."

Rackham agreed. "Why not try your friend Maddock with a photograph of Skinner? Here's
one of the Gent. You might try that too."

"I thought of that. I'm going to Enfield now. Chuck it over. By George, he was no beauty."

The two detectives parted, Rackham to inquire into the possibility that the murdered tramp had ever been in Africa, Dewar to the scene of the murder of Oliver Maddock.

He found Henry Maddock at home and was at once shown into the study. The owner of Greenlawns had altered in the few days that had elapsed since the tragic affair in his garden. His geniality and *bonhomie* had been replaced by a rather unpleasant grimness. The ready smile no longer came automatically to his lips. The inspector had a momentary feeling that this big, wealthy gentleman was really a thoroughly dangerous and savage customer, and the inspector had learnt in his twenty-five years' experience a good deal of character-reading. He noticed at his first glance the sag in the right-hand pocket of Maddock's jacket where a heavy pistol was ruining the fit of his clothes.

"Well, sir," began Maddock. "What can I do for you now?"

"Have you ever seen this man before?" asked Dewar without wasting time on preliminary courtesies. He pushed across the study table a large photograph of Aloysius Skinner and intently watched the face of his host. The latter picked up the photograph and surveyed it calmly. Not a flicker of surprise or recognition or indeed of any emotion whatsoever crossed his stern and hard face.

"Yes, I have," he said. "If I'm not greatly mistaken. It's Aloysius Skinner. I saw him once at a dinner in Pretoria. Some time just before the war. Probably April or May of 1914."

"Was that the only time you saw him?"

"Yes."

"You've a good memory for faces, Mr Maddock?"

"I have. But in this case I had an unfair advantage, Inspector. I've had plenty of opportunities for seeing Skinner's photographs since he was shot, and identifying him with the man I met in Pretoria."

"Did you ever do business with him?"

"No."

The inspector paused and then went on, "Mr Maddock, I want you to think long and carefully before you answer this next question. A great deal may hinge on your remembering accurately."

Henry Maddock's dark face grew darker during this speech, but he only said "Go ahead."

"Can you remember, at any place or at any time, however briefly or trivially, if your life crossed or touched the life of Aloysius Skinner?" Maddock's face lightened almost imperceptibly at the question and the acute inspector noticed the change. "He thought I was going to ask something else," he said to himself, "and something a dashed sight more unpleasant for him."

Maddock lay back in his chair and gazed at the ceiling. At least two minutes passed before he broke the silence, and said in a tone of quiet sincerity, "To the best of my knowledge, Inspector, our lives never crossed or touched except on that one occasion of the dinner in the club at Pretoria."

"What was the occasion?"

"I can't recall the details offhand. Roughly speaking, Skinner came out to have a look at some mines and the management stood him a dinner at the club. I wasn't at the dinner myself."

"Were you interested in those particular mines?"

"No."

"Or any concern that Skinner was in?"

"Not to my knowledge. We may have both been shareholders in the same companies, of course, but I never heard of it."

"And what were you doing in Pretoria at the time?"

There was a fraction of a second before Maddock replied, "I was prospecting."

The inspector pushed the second photograph across the table.

"Have you ever seen him before?" Maddock gazed at the photograph for a moment and then his eyebrows rose and he looked at the detective. "An ugly sort of devil. So far as I know I've never seen him."

"You don't think it might be the picture of a man you used to know, say, twelve or fourteen years ago, before he went to pieces and grew that beard?"

Maddock picked up the photograph again and stared at it intently. Then he shook his head. "Can't recall anyone who looked like that."

"Another odd question for you, sir," proceeded Dewar. "Will you take a pencil and paper and make a list of all the friends and acquaintances you've ever known whose Christian name was Sam."

Henry Maddock wrinkled his eyes and then smiled. "You're right. It is an odd question. People called Sam? Well, I suppose you've got your reasons. I'll try and do some serious thinking."

Again there was a silence until Maddock said quietly, "Lend me a pencil, will you, Inspector." Dewar handed him a stub without a word. Maddock looked at it with a touch of amusement and said, "I don't think much of the official pencil," and then began to write earnestly on a sheet of notepaper. When he had finished, he drummed thoughtfully on the table with his fingers and finally pushed the sheet across to Dewar.

"That's the lot, so far as I can remember." Dewar picked up the sheet and read aloud slowly.

"Sam Slickman. Thief. Shot in Jo'burg, Spring 1927. You're sure he was shot, Mr Maddock?"

"Quite sure, Inspector. But you can verify it. Wire the police."

"I shall, sir. Next one, 'Samuel Isaacstein, moneylender, Capetown.' Is he dead, sir?"

"No such luck. Alive and kicking and worth a million sterling."

"Not likely to be a tramp, then?"

"Not very likely," was the dry response.

"'Sam Horrabin. Boxer.' Where's he today, Mr Maddock?"

"Last I heard of him he was keeping a public house somewhere in German East."

"Anything like that?" The detective pointed at the photograph of the tramp.

"Nothing like it. Horrabin was champion in 1919, light-heavyweight."

"That certainly rules out Horrabin. Sam Blower, died of drink in 1911. Sam Smith, life sentence for murder. Sandbag Sam, ten years for robbery with violence."

The detective looked up from the sheet of notepaper and remarked mildly, "If I may say so, sir, you had a rum crowd of friends when you were in Africa."

Maddock laughed genially. "Oh, I'm a student of human nature, Dewar. I like to mix with every sort of person."

"But there you only seem to have mixed with one sort of person."

Maddock was a little disconcerted by this remark and answered, rather feebly, "Such is life, you know."

Dewar made no attempt to drive home his advantage. He put the sheet of notepaper and the photograph away in a breast pocket and got up.

"You think the same as I do about this affair, sir, don't you?" he said.

The other smiled and answered, "it would be a very clever man who knew what you were thinking, Dewar."

"I'm thinking that the bullets were not meant for your brother but were meant for you."

Maddock also got up and looked the detective straight in the eye.

"Too straight to be natural," was Dewar's thought as he saw the dark eyes gazing at him.

"I agree with you absolutely. The bullets were meant for me."

"What makes you think that?"

"Who would want to shoot my poor brother? He hadn't an enemy in the world."

"And you?" said the inspector boldly. Maddock lowered his eyes and examined his finger nails with care.

"Africa is a wild place," he murmured.

"Who was it?" asked Dewar.

"I have no idea."

"Oh, come, sir."

"It's true, Dewar. I've absolutely no idea. I know I've got enemies, lots of them. But I never knew before that I'd an enemy who wanted to kill me. That's news to me, and very unpleasant news."

"You can't give me any help?"

Maddock shook his head.

"It's in your own interest, sir," persisted Dewar.

"Of course it is. I know that as well as you do." His tone was petulant for the first time. "I've told you all I know. I haven't the faintest idea who it is or who it might be."

"Very well, sir. If you get any brain waves, I hope you'll let me know."

"Of course I will."

It was a very thoughtful inspector who left Greenlawns and proceeded to the local motor garage which had reported the visit of a stranger in search of oil and petrol about an hour before the murder of Oliver Maddock.

CHAPTER IV

Scratching for Clues in Africa and Batavia

The garage of the Star and Garter Inn was run by an intelligent man. He remembered distinctly the large Buick car which had driven up on the afternoon of Mr Maddock's tennis-party. It was particularly fixed in his mind by the fact that young Mr Maddock had been down soon after lunch to borrow a large spanner. A friend of his, the young gentleman had explained, had come over to play tennis in a new Buick and had left his tools behind. The cap of the petrol tank had jammed and they had no spanner large enough to fit it. He had lent young Mr Maddock a spanner and when he saw a big Buick turn into the yard he thought it must be the other young gentleman coming to return it.

It was, however, a stranger asking for oil and petrol. The owner of the garage, being a student of machines rather than of human nature, had paid more attention to the car than the driver. It was a six-cylinder, touring-body; painted dark-blue, with a luggage-box on the back and a fire-extinguisher of foreign pattern on the running-board. He had supplied six gallons of petrol and a gallon of oil and had watched the car move off in the direction of Greenlawns. The driver, so far as the garage-keeper could recall, was an ordinary-looking man, dressed in ordinary clothes and with an ordinary manner.

Inspector Dewar smiled at this description. "In fact, you couldn't describe a single thing about him."

The other scratched his head. "That's true," he admitted. "I'm sorry but it's true."

"Never mind," said Dewar. "You've described the car and that's always something."

No other garages in the neighbourhood had any information to offer about strange customers on the afternoon of the murder and Dewar returned to Scotland Yard with his meagre results.

On arriving at his room he found a message that Superintendent Bone wanted to see him and he went straight to his superior's office. The superintendent was engaged in his favourite occupation of lying at full length in an easy chair, staring at the wall in front of him like an overfed frog. He swivelled his bulging eyes at the Inspector as he came in, but did not move his head. It seemed as if moving his head was too much exertion.

"Sit down, Dewar," he murmured, "and tell me all the news. By the way, we've had a conference upstairs since I saw you last, and it's been decided that you and I and Rackham are to run this show. You're to take the Maddock end, Rackham to re-open his tramp stuff while I do old Skinner and what the Commissioner calls 'general co-ordination.' Co-ordination is my second name, Dewar. It suits me down to the ground. A clever chap can co-ordinate in an easy chair with his eyes shut." He winked ponderously.

"You still think the tramp has something to do with it, sir?"

Bone shook his head almost imperceptibly. It was the minimum movement that could have conveyed a negative.

"No, I don't. But it's as well to make sure. The key to the thing is in South Africa. I'm sure of that. Now your news."

Dewar described his peculiar interview with Maddock and the visit of the Buick car to the garage.

"Not much there," said Bone, "but you'll send out the usual call for the car."

"Yes, sir."

"Now about Maddock. There's been a wire from Johannesburg. Pass over that file on the table behind me. Let me see. Yes, here it is. 'Henry Maddock acquitted of manslaughter in 1911 owing to insufficient evidence but undoubtedly kicked native to death stop charged with fraudulent bankruptcy in 1913 acquitted stop chief promoter of Blavfontein Investment Corporation 1917 cleared over half million stop queer tales of trading with enemy during war but nothing proved stop origin unknown but believed wanted by Congo police before appearing Johannesburg in 1905 stop intimate friend of Rosenstein illicit diamond buyer and boxing promoter now serving twenty years stop former partner of Slingsby shot in street Durban 1918 stop an unpleasant character message ends.'"

"An unpleasant character," said Dewar, in an undertone. "By George, I should say he was."

Superintendent Bone turned over the pages of his file. "Here's another bit of information, Dewar, my lad. I went down to the offices of Imperial

Cochineal; at least when I say I went down I didn't exactly go in person. I sent Jones to go into that visit of Skinner's to Africa. He was on his own business so the officials didn't know much about it. But his private secretary knew a little. He swears that Skinner was absolutely cast-iron gilt-edge, that he was like the Bank of England. Never touched anything in the slightest bit shady. Only dealt in solid six-per-cent. stuff and got scared if he saw seven per cent. coming along because seven per cent. and shadiness went hand in hand."

"Oh, come, sir," remonstrated Dewar. His superior smiled. "Perhaps I'm exaggerating what the secretary said, but that's the impression he gave Jones. But you see the point. If Skinner was only half as upright as his secretary made him out and if Maddock is only half as big a blackguard as this wire makes him out, even so they could never have had business dealings together or even with a common third party. And it's the common third party we are looking for."

Dewar began to be slightly bewildered.

"It seems to me, sir, that you're making out a case against there being any connection between Skinner and Maddock. And yet we know there was one because the bullets are identical."

The Superintendent sat up with reluctance and tapped Dewar on the knee. "You ought to pay more attention, young man, to what I say. I've been explaining to you that there doesn't seem to be any possibility of a connection between Mr Henry Maddock and the late Chairman of Imperial Cochineal."

"But the bullets!" protested Dewar.

Superintendent Bone heaved a deep sigh. "I'm coming to the conclusion that Scotchmen become inspectors simply because they're Scotchmen. There can't be any other reason. Apply your great Caledonian intellect to the answering of this abstruse conundrum, Dewar. Was the late Aloysius Skinner born Chairman of Imperial Cochineal or did he become Chairman at a later date?"

Dewar considered this question and finally replied cautiously, "He couldn't have been born Chairman. Chairmanships aren't hereditary like monarchies."

Bone clapped him vigorously on the shoulder and boomed, "Well done, Dumbarton. Now I know why you're an inspector. We're agreed upon this, then, that it's more than likely that there was a time in the life of Skinner when he was not Chairman of Cochineal. Now, was he always so gilt-edged and upright and scrupulous? What was he before?"

"I looked at the papers two days ago. There doesn't seem to be a great deal known about his past life."

"No, Dewar, and we've got to find out about it. It seems to me that you'd better drop Maddock for a bit and try this thing from the angle of Skinner. Here's the file. Don't be put off by his reputation for honesty and financial rectitude. Find out if there ever was a period in his life when he might have—well, you know—strayed a little from the path of virtue and the Company Acts."

"What about Maddock, sir?"

"We'll leave him alone for a bit. Send a couple of men to watch the house. There's always a chance that the man who shot Oliver by mistake will come back and have another go at Henry. Tell the fellows you send down to look out for a man with a South African accent who drops diamonds all over the place," and with this parting injunction the Superintendent lay back in his chair and closed his eyes.

Dewar returned to his office and sat down to study again, and more carefully, the papers about the Skinner case. The documents were mainly connected with the murdered man's antecedents and the possibility of some old feud or grievance having been the motive of the murder. The ground had been extensively surveyed and Dewar could see no point at which new enquiries could usefully be begun. He noted down the chief dates on a writing-pad.

"Lived at Parkside, Wimbledon, since 1917. Housekeeper came at same time. Flat in Draycott Gardens from 1912 to 1917. Service flat. Kept no staff. 1910-1912 service flat in Earl's Court Road. Before 1910 domicile unknown." Dewar turned to another paper, the first entry of which read, "1910. Floated the Anglo-Batavian Cochineal Company."

"So he turned up from nowhere in 1910, took flat in Earl's Court and started this line in Cochineal," mused the detective and he turned to a paper marked "Origin."

"Hm. Born at 24 Villa Walk, Wandsworth, on April 14th, 1859. Father John, Mother Henrietta. Villa Walk pulled down in October 1894. John and Henrietta Skinner drowned in boating fatality, August 4th 1868, place unknown. No relatives left in district."

Dewar re-read the information and then went through the file till he came to a page headed "Housekeeper."

"Mrs Ann Croft, 57, engaged by answering advertisement in *Daily Telegraph*. Liked A. S.; found him a good employer. He had few friends and no enemies. Many letters came for him every day, but he always took them to the office to answer. Many with foreign stamps. Cannot remember stamps of any particular country. Spent all day at office, returning about 5.30. Almost always dined alone. Can remember no unusual incidents. A very quiet life."

Suddenly Dewar saw the weak spot in the investigation and, when he saw it, he was surprised at his own slowness and at the stupidity of the man who had made the enquiries.

He slapped the table with his open hand and then grinned to himself. "It's lucky old Bone didn't spot it," he said aloud. "He'd have ragged me for a week. I'll go and tell him."

He returned to the Superintendent's office and found him in exactly the same attitude of repose.

"About Skinner," he began, "I've found a line of enquiry that ought to help. It's been missed so far."

Bone opened his eyes wide. "I went through the file myself," he said. Dewar made no comment but went on, "Skinner founded the Anglo-Batavian in 1910. He couldn't have done that without knowing something about Batavia or cochineal or people who knew about them. What about a wire to Java, sir?"

"Good idea, Dewar," answered the Superintendent.

"I'll send one off at once, sir."

"Half-a-minute, half-a-minute. There's no necessity to do that."

"But you said it was a good idea, sir."

"So it was. Forty-eight hours ago. Here's the answer from Java. Arrived this minute." He pushed a telegraph form across to the crestfallen inspector.

"Aloysius Skinner appeared in Java 1907 left 1909 stop no details available," Dewar read. "That doesn't carry us much further."

The Superintendent nodded. "Why do you suppose there are no details?" he asked suddenly.

"Too long ago, sir," answered Dewar promptly.

"Only twenty years."

"There seem to be very few details about him wherever we go," Dewar grumbled.

"Come on, Dewar, have a guess at it," urged the Superintendent. "It's a tropical climate out there."

"All his contemporaries are dead," hazarded Dewar.

"Oh, not so bad as all that."

"Then they've all come home by now."

"Well done, Dewar. You're improving. If Skinner was a man of forty or forty-five when he went out he would be more likely to associate with the seniors in the headquarters offices rather than with the young fellows on the actual plantations. By now all the seniors will have retired and the men who were juniors in 1909 never knew him."

Dewar seized his papers. "I'll start at once, sir. I'll find a planter who knew Skinner if I have to drag him from his grave."

"From his Club would be better," murmured Superintendent Bone, closing his eyes.

CHAPTER V

Investigating the Background of Mr Aloysius Skinner

For the next two days the investigations were pursued along the several different lines, each detective working his own line and reporting progress to Superintendent Bone, who sat like a vast spider in his room at Scotland Yard.

Inspector Dewar went from Club to Club, from address to address, the clubs being mostly in Piccadilly, the addresses mostly in South and West Kensington, in search of ex-planters of tea, coffee, or rubber who knew Aloysius Skinner in Java.

Inspector Rackham returned to the police-stations on the Berkhampstead – Banbury Road, where indignant tramps had been rounded up a second time to answer his questions.

Two plain-clothes men watched unobtrusively the outside of Greenlawns and one of them was savagely attacked by a half-wild Alsatian dog, which neighbours declared to be a newcomer to the Maddock establishment. The house itself was no longer the scene of gay tennis-parties. Even in the day-time all the shutters on the ground and first floors were kept shut and there was no sign of the master of the house. The son and daughter had vanished.

A vigilant search was maintained for the dark-blue Buick with the foreign fire-extinguisher, while the police of Johannesburg received a second long telegram asking them to verify the statements made by Henry Maddock in his most recent interview with Inspector Dewar.

Towards the end of the second day Dewar ran to earth the man he was looking for. He found an old rubber-grower who not only remembered Skinner's visit but had done business with him. More important still, he actually dug out of one of twenty-four tin trunks, all filled with letters and papers, a letter which he had received from Skinner before the latter's arrival in Java.

The old planter explained that he never destroyed a letter in his life and never forgot a face and never forgave an enemy, by God, sir. He refused to discuss business until Dewar had accepted the biggest whisky and soda and the blackest cigar he had ever seen, and it was not until the detective was in full swing with both drink and smoke that the old man began his rambling and irrelevant reminiscences of life in the East. Dewar had to sit and listen as patiently as he could. Twice he tried to hurry the veteran and was twice rewarded with an excursus into modern manners compared with true old-fashioned courtesy. The search for the letters was even more exasperating as the planter repeatedly came on some document that reminded him of long-forgotten episodes in the lives of long-forgotten planters, games of polo, record crops, swimming-races, the fidelity of native servants or sensational 'hands' at poker. At last he found the precious letter, carried it over to the light to make certain and then handed it with a courtly bow to the eager detective.

The paper was dry and yellow, the ink faded, but Dewar could easily read the small, neat handwriting. It was dated December 15th, 1906, and beside the date were the words that Dewar was looking for, the address from which it was written: 240 Holborn, London, England. The letter ran as follows:

"Dear Sir,
I enclose the copy of a letter of introduction to you from our mutual friend Mr Van Doone. The original letter I hope to present in person at your office as I am sailing shortly for the East Indies. With your permission I will acquaint you of my arrival in Singapore. Until then, sir,
I remain, Your obdt. servant,
A. SKINNER.

Alex. Elphinston, Esq."

Dewar read it through twice and then turned to the ex-planter. "And Mr Van Doone?" he asked. Mr Elphinston puckered up a brow that was almost as shiny and as yellow as the letter.

"Old Van Doone?" he said. "A nice fellow."

"Where is he now?"

"Gone to the other Van Doones, gathered to his fathers, these twenty years."

"Mr Elphinston," said Dewar seriously. "Do you think there's any chance of that letter of introduction being in one of those tin boxes?"

"Any chance?" echoed the ancient in a voice of withering scorn. "If I received it, it's in one of the boxes. I never threw away a letter—"

"Quite so, of course," interrupted Dewar hastily. "Do you think you could possibly find it?"

"Not today," answered Mr Elphinston. "I'm tired now. But tomorrow I will. Come round at the same time tomorrow. Fill your glass."

Dewar succeeded in declining the offer and took a cab to 240 Holborn.

It was the number, as he had expected, of a large and dingy building, a dark, rabbit-warren of countless offices. In an even darker and dingier basement lurked an elderly caretaker, and it was to her that Dewar turned for information. He had only one question to ask and it was promptly answered. The rents of the building were collected by Messrs. Hope, Charteris & Batten, Surveyors and Estate Agents, Great Cumberland Place. The Inspector drove to the surveyors and was shown into the office of one of the partners of the firm, a Mr Dennis. The walls of the office were lined with square, black boxes bearing, in white paint, names so illustrious that Dewar blinked with awe and dazzlement. The manner of Mr Dennis was almost as dazzling. It was slow, urbane, bland, ceremonious. It conveyed the impression that upon those broad and morning-coated shoulders rested the burdens of marquises and dukes, even, perhaps, of personages more exalted still. He received the inspector with the profoundest courtesy, turning aside for an instant to give an instruction to an accountant as if the accountant had been at the very least a baronet or a law-lord.

Dewar explained his business. Could he see the rent-roll of 240 Holborn for the years 1906 and 1907?

Mr Dennis pressed a bell and then bowed. "I wish all our little problems were as easy of solution as that, Mr.—er—Commissioner—er—"

"Inspector, sir."

"Ah, yes. Of course. You must forgive my ignorance, Inspector. Ah, Mr Bernard. Would it be troubling you too much to ask you to step down to the vaults and bring up the rent-rolls of 240 Holborn for the years 1906 and 1907, I fear you may find it rather dusty down there."

The young man addressed as Mr Bernard was an alert youth of about sixteen years of age, and he shot out of the room with a speed that seemed to distress, very faintly but perceptibly, the Victorian serenity of Mr Dennis. He sighed very slightly and murmured, "It is an age of speed and progress, sir."

Silence settled on the room. Dewar had nothing to say and Mr Dennis appeared to be dreaming of a past and more leisurely age. A brisk knock at the door aroused him and the office-boy darted into the room bearing two large ledgers.

"Two-four-o Holborn '06 and '07, sir," he observed briskly, and laid them before Mr Dennis.

"I am extremely obliged to you, Mr Bernard. Thank you very much, thank you very much indeed." The office boy vanished like a pantomime demon, and Mr Dennis waved to the ledgers. "And now, sir."

"The name I am looking for is Skinner, sir. Aloysius Skinner."

Mr Dennis was startled for an instant. "Dear me. You don't say so. Do you mean Mr Aloysius Skinner who——"

"Yes, sir."

"Dear me! How very interesting! A remarkable man, inspector. A very remarkable man." He was running a finger down the index as he spoke. "A sad end. Tragic affair. And you think he may have had one of our offices at one time. Sampson, Sandringham Braces Company, Scandinavian Wood-pulp, Sims & Ratchett, Sorrel & Sons, no, he's not in that list. But wait one moment, Inspector. Because his name is not in the rent-roll it does not follow that he did not have one of our offices." He rose and walked slowly across the thick carpet to a safe which was hidden away behind a revolving bookcase, unlocked it and extracted a small, leather-bound volume.

"Our private 'Who's Who,' Inspector. I've no doubt you have something of the sort at Scotland Yard."

"Something of the sort," conceded Dewar with an ironical smile that was completely lost on the dignified Surveyor and Estate Agent. "Now, sir, here we are," proceeded the latter. "Skinner, A., Managing Director of the Colonial Development Company. Three year lease of office number 37. March, 1905 to March, 1908. References, Childs Bank and Whittier, Lampton & Whittier, 314 Essex Street, Strand."

"Solicitors, I presume," said Dewar.

"Probably. I don't recall the name. They must be in a very small way, if indeed they survive."

Mr Dennis replaced his "Who's Who" in the safe, came back to his ledgers, and turned up the Colonial Development Company.

"Nothing more of interest," he said. "They banked with Childs, paid the rent regularly and gave up the offices on quarter day in March, 1908."

"I am greatly obliged to you, sir," said the Inspector, but Mr Dennis insisted that the obligation was the other way round. He blandly refused to listen to thanks or to agree to the suggestion that his valuable time had been wasted.

"In my profession, Inspector, we come frequently into contact with the law of property, of landlord and tenant, of probate and so on. But;

never before have I come into contact with the criminal law and it is a profoundly interesting experience." He personally led the inspector to the door, bowed him out and returned to his ducal and more than ducal tin boxes.

Dewar returned to Scotland Yard, not dissatisfied with the result of his day's work. The life of Aloysius Skinner had been carried back two years and there were three distinct threads, any or all of which might be reasonably expected to carry it back still further. There were the records of Childs Bank, the history of the Colonial Development Company and the letter of introduction from Mr Van Doone.

The most promising of the three seemed at first sight to be the Colonial Development Company. There was every possibility of it having some connection with Africa. And that, Dewar reminded himself, was the primary object of the investigation. Seated on the top of a bus, he ran over the dates in his mind. Henry Maddock went to Africa, according to his own story, in 1888. It was not until 1905 that he first appeared in Johannesburg. It was thought that part of the intervening years had been spent in Belgian Congo. He made a note to telegraph to Brussels for information. From 1905 until 1919 he seemed to have remained in British South Africa. During almost the identical period Skinner's whereabouts seemed to be accounted for. Two years in Holborn, two in Java, and then an increasingly well-known figure in the City of London from the time of his return until his death. It appeared to Dewar to be almost conclusive that the connection between Skinner and Maddock must lie in the years before 1905 or after 1919. The latter contingency could be ruled out. Secretive though the late Chairman of Imperial Cochineal had been, he could hardly have concealed from his office staff, his private secretaries, his board of directors, transactions so important that it was worth while for some third party to commit two murders in order to suppress them. The crucial period was unquestionably the years before 1905 when Henry Maddock was a wild and unscrupulous young adventurer on the African Continent and Aloysius Skinner was—what? Dewar lit his pipe and wondered.

CHAPTER VI

The Extraordinarily Quiet Life of Mr Aloysius Skinner

Inspector Dewar was a Scotsman. Born on a farm in Dumbartonshire, the eldest son of a family of seven sons and three daughters, he had from an early age helped his father to provide for the rest of the family. His official education had, therefore, been somewhat neglected as he had left school at the first instant permitted by the law. But his real education had continued in his spare moments during the day and every evening on his return home from work. His father taught him practically simultaneously how to drive a plough and to read Livy, so that at the age of nineteen he was able to take the usual plunge that young Scotsmen take. He borrowed sufficient money for the railway fare and went to London. On arriving, he went straight to the house of a Dumbartonshire acquaintance who had taken the plunge successfully a few years earlier and lodged with him for six weeks. He employed the time in finding out the qualifications and conditions for entry into the Metropolitan Police Force, and then presented himself as a candidate. His fine physique and his "book-learning" caught the fancy of the authorities and shortly afterwards he was accepted as a recruit. His rise was unspectacular but steady, and he owed his Inspectorship to his dogged courage, his attention to detail, his persistence and his capacity for studying the theory of detection, rather than to any particularly brilliant feats of daring or intellect. He had no trace of Highland dash or instability. He stuck to facts and pursued a case to the bitter end. The result was that he was trusted by his superiors and respectfully and affectionately chaffed by his juniors. He was a bachelor and had no recreations or hobbies outside his profession. When he was in charge of a case, he thought of the case and dreamt of the case. It practically took possession of him for twenty-four hours a day.

On returning to his office from his visit to Mr Dennis, the inspector first of all sent a telegram to the Headquarters of the Belgian Police in

Brussels asking for enquiries to be made in the Belgian territories in Africa. Then, after a moment's consideration, he sent duplicates to the French, Portuguese, Italian, and Spanish police. Maddock might have turned up in any of these obscure colonies at one time or another. Dewar then pulled a large atlas from one of the drawers in his table and turned to Africa.

"Hm. That pretty well covers it," he said to himself. "All except Abyssinia and Liberia. Probably no police there, anyway."

The telephone on his desk rang and he picked up the receiver.

"Rackham speaking," said the voice. "Can I come up and see you?"

"Certainly," said Dewar. He put down the telephone and picked up a bundle of reports that had been awaiting his return and glanced through them. Most of them were reports of failure to trace the Buick car. "I never thought we'd get very much out of that anyway," he muttered, and then Rackham came in.

"Any luck?" he asked at once.

"Yes and no," said Rackham. "I had all those tramps pulled in during the last forty-eight hours and I went through them all again. Not one of them had ever heard of Stuck-up Sam ever being abroad. He never said a word about it and he never talked about it."

"Of course, that's not proof one way or the other."

"No. But I came across one rather curious thing. One of these tramps had been in South Africa. He was a trooper in a Yeomanry regiment, fought in the Boer War, settled out there afterwards, came to grief and drank himself to blazes. That's his yarn, anyway. Now he knew this Stuck-up Sam well, and he swears he never was in Africa. They worked a beat together for five weeks in 1922 and this fellow says he couldn't have failed to discover if Sam had ever been in Africa."

"That's probably true enough," commented Dewar. "What was this fellow like? Anything like Sam?"

"Not a bit. He must have been a fine big man once. Broad shoulders and fair hair."

"In this case you never can tell, apparently. A man who could take Oliver Maddock for Henry Maddock could do anything in the mistaking line. Did your ex-trooper friend have any idea that he was the real objective of the murderer?"

"I asked him," said Rackham with a grin. "It gave him no end of a shock. But he swore he hadn't an enemy in the world. And I must say, Dewar, I was inclined to believe him. After he'd got over the first unpleasant surprise he didn't seem in the least afraid or worried."

"So we're not much further along that direction," said Dewar.

"Well, I wish you joy of it," said Rackham. "I'm through with it."

"What! Are you being taken off?"

"Yes. I've done all there is to be done with the tramp. I'm going down to Penzance tonight on an arsenic case. Weed-killer and life-insurance stuff. You know the sort of thing."

"I hope you enjoy it," answered Dewar absently, and then added, "I say. Van Doone is a Dutch name and of course South Africa is full of Dutchmen."

"So is Java," replied Rackham.

"That's true. This Van Doone might be the link that connects Java, Africa, Maddock and Skinner."

"And the tramp?"

"Ah! The tramp. I'm getting a little sceptical about that tramp. He doesn't seem to fit into things somehow."

"Nothing seems to fit anywhere. Good luck," said Rackham with a laugh and he went out.

Dewar tidied away his papers, locked his desk and walked slowly homewards. He was famous among the junior staff at Scotland Yard, for being the last of the Inspectors to leave in the evening and the first to arrive in the morning. He slept with a telephone beside his bed and was never grumpy or snappy if called half a dozen times in the course of the night after twenty hours on his feet, tramping hot, hard pavements.

He was not in the least annoyed, therefore, on being woken just after midnight with the news that the driver of the Buick had been detained and was at that moment on his way to Headquarters. In ten minutes, Dewar was dressed and mounted upon the ancient and rusty bicycle which he reserved for nocturnal expeditions after the hours of trains, trams and buses and on business which did not justify the expense to the public purse of a taxi-cab. In the deserted streets it did not take him long to reach the Yard from his small villa in the Kennington Park Road. The detained man had arrived only a few minutes before and was led straight into Dewar's room.

He was a young man, not more than twenty or twenty-one years of age, with healthy, pink cheeks, negligent but well-cut clothes and an air of easy assurance that is not common in people who are being detained at Scotland Yard on suspicion of being concerned in a murder case. "Wrong again," thought Dewar instantly, as the young man entered. Five minutes' conversation was sufficient to confirm his fears. The youth gave a full and frank account of his movements on the day of the murder, quoted half a dozen well-known Shropshire families who would give evidence of his identity as heir to Shipton Manor in that county, seemed to be delighted at the story he would have to tell when he returned to Trinity College, Cambridge, and begged in vain to have his fingerprints taken. Before leaving he succeeded in extorting a promise from the half-amused and half-reluctant Dewar that he would personally conduct him over Scotland Yard on some future and more suitable occasion.

"That's that," said Dewar thoughtfully, as he remounted his bicycle and pedalled slowly along the Embankment towards the Vauxhall Bridge Road.

The interruption to his night's rest made no difference to his capacity for early rising and he was back in his office just before eight o'clock struck. A telegram from South Africa lay on his desk. "This confirms," it ran, "maddock's statement *re* slickman isaacstein sandbag smith stop am enquiring about blower stop have wired walfisch bay for information re horrabin message ends."

After two hours' hard routine work Dewar was ready to pursue the search. His first visit was to Somerset House to investigate the affairs of the Colonial Development Company. It had been registered in the autumn of 1904 with a nominal capital of £50,000, of which £10,000 had been subscribed. The Chairman of the Board of Directors was Ludovic Van Doone and the Managing Director was A. Skinner. No other names appeared in the registration. The company was merged in 1908 into the Far-East Produce Company and again the Chairman was Ludovic Van Doone, the Managing Director A. Skinner. In 1909 the Far-East Produce Company was absorbed by the Anglo-Batavian Company, which, in its turn, in 1915, became a subsidiary concern of what afterwards was called the Imperial Cochineal Company. From 1909 the name of Van Doone dropped out.

The inspector's next visit was to the Headquarters of the colossal joint-Stock Bank, which had absorbed Childs Bank. The assistant manager, who received him, promised to have the account of the Colonial Development Company ready for his examination if he would return in two hours. Dewar filled in the time with a bus ride to Essex Street. The journey was fruitless. Messrs. Whittier, Lampton & Whittier had long since vanished, not only from Essex Street, but from the universe itself. Not even the oldest inhabitant of the block of offices at number 314 could recall the name. A firm of law stationers in Chancery Lane obligingly delved into ancient books of reference and extracted the information that the firm of Whittier, Lampton & Whittier, solicitors, had been wound up on the bankruptcy of the last surviving partner in 1912. The partner's name had been Alfred Lampton.

Dewar sauntered slowly down Fleet Street. He was elbowed and jostled by the hurrying, breathless crowds that never seem to have a moment to spare in that breathless street. Hatless clerks, lawyers, journalists, typists, all had one thing in common. They were all in a hurry. Dewar stopped on the kerb and looked absently at an elderly man who was hastening out of an insurance office with a roll of papers in his hand. "If you dropped down dead," murmured the detective, "I wonder how many people could tell me what you were doing twenty-five years ago. I wonder if anybody knows. This is a most confounded business." He glanced at his watch and resumed his stroll, reaching the Bank exactly as the two hours were up. The account of the Colonial Development Company was ready for him.

As he had expected, the account consisted entirely of expenditure except for the deposit at the beginning of £10,000 and the periodical interest on the varying amount that was kept on deposit account.

"The company doesn't seem to have done a roaring trade," Dewar observed to the clerk who was in charge of the ledgers. "Let's see where the money went to." He ran his fingers down the expenditure column, pausing at each item of any considerable size. "Hundred and thirty to Whiteleys. That was office funiture. Hope, Charteris & Batten—rent, of course. Skinner's salary. Dividend at 7 per cent. to Val Doone—how did they pay a dividend when they did no business—Skinner's salary again, rent—well, this is a most extraordinary thing."

Dewar looked at the clerk. "What would you say to a company that took offices and paid a manager and then did nothing else?"

"I should say, sir, that it was jolly queer," replied the clerk.

"So should I," returned the inspector, taking up his hat and stick. "Thank you very much for your trouble."

An underground train conveyed him swiftly from the city to Kensington, and he found the yellow and ancient Mr Elphinston in high good humour.

"You said I wouldn't find that letter of introduction," he croaked with a venerable gaiety. "Oh, yes, you did. You may pretend that you didn't, but you did. But I've found it. Every letter I've ever had is in one of those boxes. Did I tell you about young Crink Anderson—we called him Crink because, because—now why the devil did we call him Crink? I know the reason as well as I know my own name. Oh, yes, it was because he came from Harrogate. Or was it Taunton? Anyway, it was in sixty-two."

"But the letter of introduction," interposed Dewar skilfully as the Malayan Nestor paused for breath.

"Here it is. I always find everything. The very words that Van Doone wrote." He handed over another yellow faded paper.

Dewar, before reading it, asked, "What do you know of Van Doone, sir?"

"Old Van Doone," answered the old man with energy. "A damned rich old Dutchman. Not a bad fellow for a Dutchman. But rich. Damned rich. Dead now. Dead twenty years or more. I knew him in Singapore. He had big ideas."

"Where did he live?"

"Live? Everywhere. London, Rotterdam, Paris. A big man. Ask the Dutch Consulate."

Mr Elphinston launched a long anecdote of some stupendous gamble which had taken place fifty years before on some up-country plantation, and under cover of the story Dewar read the letter of introduction. It was dated December 1st, 1906, from 240 Holborn, and ran simply:

Dear Mr Elphinston.
    This is to introduce my friend Mr A. Skinner. I know you will like him. With kind regards,
        Your obedient servant,
            L. Van Doone.

Dewar fled as soon as was compatible with good manners and proceeded to the Dutch Consulate. The office, however, was closed, and he was asked to return on the following morning. All the senior officials were at some function or other and the juniors could not help him. From the consulate he went to a telephone-box and looked up the name of Lampton. It was a forlorn hope, but it was one of Dewar's maxims never to look for anyone's address until he was certain that it was not in the telephone-book. His experience had proved to him the extraordinary variety of people who are on the London telephone. Sure enough there was an Alfred Lampton, described as a Turf Commission Agent, 291 Shaftesbury Avenue. "From bankrupt to bookie," murmured Dewar. "I wonder if it's the same man. A hundred to one against. But it would make a good title for a book." He grinned to himself and ran after a bus that was going in the direction of Shaftesbury Avenue. Number 291 was a building that had a number of brass plates at the entrance. Among the names was Alfred Lampton, Turf Commission Agent, whose office, apparently, was situated on the fourth floor. Dewar walked up the four flights of stone stairs, knocked at and entered a door marked "A. Lampton. Enquiries."

The room was a small one and contained a girl with almost unbelievably flaxen hair, who was pounding away at a typewriter, and a pimply-faced youth of Jewish extraction, whose pointed patent-leather shoes were as shiny as his brilliantined hair. He was sitting on the edge of the typist's table, studying a racing periodical. Both looked up at Dewar's entrance and both stared at him a little apprehensively. The girl stopped typing. "Yes, sir?" she said.

"Can I see Mr Lampton?" asked Dewar, nodding his head towards an inner door marked "Private."

"Have you an appointment?"

"No."

"Name, please?"

"Dewar."

"And the nature of your business?"

"Private."

The girl slipped through the inner door in such a way that Dewar could see nothing of the room beyond. "She's done that before," thought the detective admiringly.

After a brief interval the typist reappeared with the same deftness and said, "Please state the nature of your business."

"Thank you, Miss," said Dewar genially, and stepped across to the door marked "Private." It was locked. "Quick work," he observed, and ran back to the landing outside the door marked "Enquiries." There was no one on the stairs. The inner room of Mr Alfred Lampton had a door on to the landing, but it also was locked and Dewar returned to the "Enquiries."

"Here! What are you playing at?" demanded the young man in loud tones. "Any more of this funny stuff and I'll send for the police."

"Don't worry, lad," said Dewar. "I am the police." He flicked a card on to the table. The youth picked it up, whistled and handed it to the peroxide damsel. Then he turned cringingly to Dewar. "Sorry, guv'nor. Duty's duty. What do you want?"

"A word with the boss."

The youth knocked at the inner door and shouted, "Cop to see you."

There was an interval of at least two minutes before the door opened and a voice called out, "Show him in."

Mr Alfred Lampton was a middle-aged gentleman of distasteful appearance. His clothes were a mixture of flashiness and seediness, his manner a mixture of obsequiousness and defiance. He smiled an ingratiating smile as he pushed forward a chair and at the same moment shot a shifty and venomous glance at the detective out of the corner of his eyes. "I wouldn't care to be in the power of this sportsman," thought Dewar as he sat down.

"Well, what do you want?" began Mr Lampton, his eyes resting everywhere but on the detective's face and his fingers nervously playing with a penholder. He seemed to be a little out of breath.

"Mr Lampton?" asked Dewar.

"Yes."

"Late of Whittier, Lampton & Whittier, solicitors, of Essex Street?"

"No. That was my father."

"Your father? And may I ask, sir, is your father—er——?"

"No. He died in 1918." The man was already beginning to regain his self-confidence. "Did your father leave any papers about his affairs when he was a solicitor?"

Mr Lampton considered this question carefully before replying.

"A few," he admitted at last.

"May I see them?" asked Dewar.

"They're all destroyed," replied Mr Lampton, in the defiant tone of a man who expects to be called a liar and is not in a position to resent it. "I burnt them after my father died."

"There might be a reward for information," said Dewar pensively, but the Commission Agent refused to be drawn. He fixed his beady eyes for a moment on the detective's face and said nothing.

"All the papers are burnt?" pursued Dewar.

"All of them," answered Mr Lampton.

"There wasn't anything about a company called the Colonial Development, was there? Or a man called Skinner? Ah, well! It all happened too long ago." Dewar picked up his hat. "Sorry to have troubled you, Mr Lampton. Don't get up. I can find my own way out."

Disregarding the Commission Agent's grubby hand, Dewar went out and descended the stairs. He halted at the bottom, pulled a notebook from his pocket and turned to the section headed B. On the page at the top of which stood the word "Blackmail," he wrote, "Alfred Lampton, Turf Commission Agent, 291 Shaftesbury Avenue," and then, methodically turning to section L, he wrote, "Lampton, Alfred, Turf Commission Agent, 291 Shaftesbury Avenue, Blackmailer."

From Shaftesbury Avenue, Dewar proceeded by tube, underground and omnibus to the small house in Cambridge Road, Putney, where Mrs Ann Croft, late housekeeper to Mr Aloysius Skinner, had retired since the death of her employer.

Mrs Croft was at home. Indeed, it was the lady herself who opened the door. Dewar explained his errand and apologized for adding to the number of questions which the police had already asked her. But Mrs Croft was not in the least annoyed. Mr Skinner had been a good employer and had treated her generously both during his life and in his will and Mrs Croft declared that she would do everything in her power to help the authorities to track down the murderer.

Dewar was pleasantly surprised with the former housekeeper's quiet intelligence. She was neither talkative nor stolid, but concentrated solely on answering his questions.

"I want you to think of the early days," began Dewar, when he was comfortably seated in an armchair in Mrs Croft's parlour, "when you first went as housekeeper to Mr Skinner. Was there anything that struck you as peculiar about the household?"

"Only the quietness of it, sir. There were hardly any visitors and Mr Skinner hardly ever went out."

"He was a friendless sort of man?"

"He was, sir."

"But though he had no friends he also had no enemies?"

"None that I know of."

"Or relations?"

"He often told me that he had no relations in the world. His father and mother were drowned on a Bank Holiday when he was a child."

"Now, Mrs Croft, you must have known that big house at Wimbledon better than most people. In all your time there did you ever come across evidence of Mr Skinner having been afraid of anyone? I mean did you ever come across a pistol, or a loaded stick? Were there burglar-alarms or special bolts or anything of the kind?"

"Never, sir."

"But you would have known if they'd been there?"

"I used to spring clean every year and I couldn't have missed them unless they'd been hidden in some place I didn't know of. There certainly were no burglar-alarms."

"About the people who used to come to the house," proceeded the detective, "I understand you to say that there were very few of them."

"Very few."

"But there were some?"

"The one who came oftenest was Mr Skinner's secretary from the office. Sometimes he brought a box of papers for Mr Skinner to see, but it didn't happen more than three or four times a year. Then there was Sir Henry

Hutton. He was a partner of Mr Skinner's, I think, and another man from the office, a Mr Brett."

"Those were business friends. Had Mr Skinner no personal friends? Did no one ever visit him who seemed to be on intimate terms with him?"

"Intimate terms? No one, sir."

"And Mr Skinner never said much about his past life?"

"No, sir. Very little. He was not a talkative gentleman."

Dewar sighed and Mrs Croft was quick to notice it. "I'm sorry, sir, not to be able to help more. I would if I could, God knows. But Mr Skinner was queer, sir, in that way. He hardly ever talked, and so, of course, I know very little of interest about him."

The Inspector declined a cup of tea and returned to Scotland Yard. On his desk lay a telegram from the town of Alberta, Canada. "Details of Skinner's murder just received stop last year similar cardboards marked one and two were found on scene of double murder in this state stop does this interest you if so will forward details."

"Does this interest us?" said Dewar aloud. "I should say it does."

CHAPTER VII

The Canadian Connection, Numbers One and Two

In the interval of waiting for the vitally important telegram from Alberta, Inspector Dewar followed up the slender clues on which he was working. There was no development at Enfield. Greenlawns remained silent and shuttered. The attempt to trace the car, which had driven away immediately after the shooting of Oliver Maddock, failed. The footprints in the shrubbery, the marks of a rope ladder on the wall and the small patch of oil on the hardshining surface of the lane outside were equally valueless. No one came forward who had seen suspicious characters in the lane or a waiting car.

The sergeant who was in charge of these enquiries reported a complete failure to Superintendent Bone. The Superintendent rolled a waggish eye at his junior and said mildly, "I'm not surprised. But it looks well to say we've done it. Those folks upstairs, you know."

The chief of the Essen police telegraphed that the firm of Krupps, in his area, was manufacturing air-pistols which would fire a bullet of the size that had killed the two men. He added that they were turning out five thousand of them a month.

The Dutch Consulate provided some information about Van Doone and, at Dewar's request, telephoned to Holland for further details. Van Doone had been a distinguished chemist. Formerly professor of chemistry in the University of Leyden, he had abandoned teaching for research and had led the life of a recluse in his laboratory for many years. He was comparatively advanced in life when he emerged from his seclusion and plunged into the world of commerce and practical affairs. So much the Consul knew off hand. Van Doone had died a rich and well-known man.

A few hours later this sketch of the Dutchman's career was supplemented by telephone from The Hague. At the age of fifty-three Van Doone had suddenly thrown himself and his vast chemical knowledge into the financial market. A rich man by inheritance, he quickly trebled and quadrupled his fortune and, when he died in 1909 at the age of sixty-two, he bequeathed over a quarter of a million pounds to Dutch charities and all his patents to his English manager and partner, Aloysius Skinner. No one knew or seemed to know how or when Van Doone and Skinner first became acquainted, but it was the generally held opinion that the Englishman had managed the finances of the various Van Doone enterprises while the Dutchman supplied the chemical knowledge. In answer to a last enquiry by Dewar the Consul's informant at the Hague was positive that Van Doone's name had never been publicly associated with South Africa. He had always faced, as it were, towards the Dutch East Indies.

Dewar pondered over this information and decided to lay it before the Superintendent at once.

"It makes one or two things clearer, sir," he said to Bone after he had told the story, "but I'm hanged if they're the things we want clearer. It doesn't take us any further back in Skinner's life. It's a confoundedly irritating case," he added, with a rare touch of annoyance.

The Superintendent raised his eyebrows slightly. "Keep your temper, young Dumbartonshire," he remarked. "The news from Canada will solve all our troubles, I expect. You're right about this Van Doone story. It explains some things that don't matter. For instance Skinner's wonderful rise was based on those patents. And that wild goose development company of yours in Holborn. That must have been a dummy company, masking some financial manoeuvre elsewhere. They must have had rather fun, those two. An inventor with money of his own can have no end of a time if he goes about it properly." He broke off and then added seriously, "it's a most extraordinary thing that we can't find even the shadow of a link between Skinner and Maddock. Well, well, we must just wait for the cable from Alberta."

"I can't see at the moment, sir, that there's anything I can do in the meantime," said Dewar. "Every line of enquiry seems to have come to an end."

The Superintendent lay back in his chair. "Where was Skinner when he met Van Doone? Check the dates, Dewar. Van Doone was fifty-three when he began to raid the financial pigeons and he was sixty-two when he died in 1909. So he started in 1900."

"That's right, sir."

"Presumably, though it's not certain, he met Skinner at about that time. He wouldn't have met him before, if he was such a hermit, and it couldn't have been much later."

"Why not, sir?" asked Dewar.

The Superintendent sighed comically and Dewar regretted that he had spoken.

"The scientific hermit suddenly becomes a financier in 1900. Later we know that he had engaged an English manager of extreme astuteness. It is probable, though as I say not absolutely certain, that the two events synchronised. We don't know how they met and probably never will. But we can at least guess that it was not much later than 1900."

He paused again and gazed at the ceiling. Dewar thought it wisest not to venture another remark. At last Bone broke the silence.

"Let it wait, Dewar, till we hear from Alberta. If nothing comes of that, which God forbid, we must have a shot at the meeting of Skinner and Van Doone. It's faintly possible that both of them and Skinner met during the South African War——"

"That's an idea, sir," exclaimed Dewar.

"Thank you very much," replied the Superintendent in a tone of profound seriousness. "In the meantime you might step down to 224b Grosvenor House and see what has happened to her ladyship's diamonds. It'll take your mind off for a bit. It's a combined 'cat' and safe-cracker job. There aren't many of them about so it shouldn't be very difficult. Look up young Alf Horner. He was practising on an old drainpipe in his backyard last time I heard of him. And on your way out ask Jones about that ornament of Chicago who arrived lately. I've forgotten his name. Jones will know who I mean."

For the next two days, Dewar was busy calling on old friends in East and South-East London. The opening of Lord Prenderling's safe had been done in a manner characteristic of only the upper ten of safe-crackers. Of those ten, three were in prison and two were too old to climb a forty-five foot drain-pipe with an oxyacetylene apparatus on their backs. That left five of the "masters" to be accounted for and Dewar accounted for them. Four had undoubted alibis. The fifth had vanished. Dewar returned to headquarters and made his report. From that moment the expert was no longer required and the System took charge.

On the third day, a telegram arrived from Alberta and Dewar was summoned to the Superintendent's office.

"There you are, Dewar," said Bone briskly, throwing several sheets of paper down on the table. "What do you make of that? Sit down and take your time." The telegram was as follows : "Reference your inquiries Stonepipe Ranch murders of May 14, 1927 stop Edgar Rice fifty seven and George Wilton fifty one murdered by unknown persons stop former shot and marked one latter axed and marked two stop murdered men were partners having immigrated from England before the war and both greatly respected and liked in district stop had no enemies and motive for crime was not discovered stop Rice and Wilton were from south of England and were understood to have farmed in Kent and Hampshire stop Rice widower and Wilton bachelor full report follows by mail message ends."

"Well?" said Bone when Dewar looked up from the telegram. "What about that?"

"Looks like the same series, sir, doesn't it?

"It looks very like the same series, though of course we must be on our guard against coincidences. But we'll assume, anyway, that it's the same." The Superintendent's voice dropped and he meandered along quietly. "Of course there are the numbers, which may mean nothing. Then there's the absence of motive. That's the same in all five cases. What's the point of hacking people about with axes if you haven't got a pretty strong reason for it? There's not a shadow of motive for any of these five cases. Then there's another curious feature. All the murdered men were past middle age. Skinner was seventy. The tramp, if that Prayer Book really was his, was sixty-six. And even if it wasn't he was over sixty. Henry Maddock is fifty-five and now these two Canadians were fifty-seven and fifty-one. That's a link between them all and it helps to confirm our notion that whatever it was that started this business took place before 1905. That problem in geometry, Dewar, ought to be easier now. We've got five lines now. Where they meet is the end of our problem."

"I can't get two of them to meet, let alone five," said Dewar.

"We'll get it this time, my boy. Rice and Wilton, south-country farmers before the war. Find them for me and let me know when you've found them."

A circular inquiry addressed to all chief constables in the southern counties met with a quick result. Edgar Rice and George Wilton had worked as farm labourers on a farm called Spinneys, near Petworth, in Sussex. Several people in the neighbourhood remembered them well, including the proprietor of Spinneys who had employed them. Dewar at once arranged that the local police should collect every available man, woman or child who remembered the men and that he himself should proceed to Petworth to interview them.

There were altogether nine inhabitants who were able to give information and Dewar found them duly marshalled in the police station. He took them one by one and from their various and rambling stories he was able to piece together a very fair sketch of the lives and characters of the two men as they had appeared to the inhabitants of the district.

In the first place, Rice and Wilton had arrived in the neighbourhood in 1909. From the very beginning they had been a centre of interest. They were penniless but had obviously come from better things. They were good looking, well-set-up fellows and it was a great surprise when they applied for, and received, jobs at Spinneys as ordinary farmhands. But they knew their business and did their work well. There was a good deal of uncertainty as to their place of origin. Of the nine informants, three thought that the men had come from beyond Winchester, two had always believed them to be from Southampton, three had never considered the problem and one was positive that they came from the Midlands.

But on one thing all nine were unanimous. Rice and Wilton had not mingled with the local folk. They had kept themselves to themselves and did a lot of work in the corner of the bar parlour of the Rose and Thistle with bits of paper and stumps of pencils. It was generally thought that they were working out schemes to get rich. But the village never knew for certain, for the day after Harvest Sunday, 1911, the two men calmly announced that they were leaving for Canada and walked unconcernedly off down the Southampton road with their worldly goods on their backs and were never seen again in Petworth, After the ninth and last citizen had finished his tale and departed to the public house opposite, Dewar sat down and looked at his notes. There was not very much that was helpful. The period covered did not stretch back to the vital years before 1905 and Dewar gloomily admitted to himself that tracing the lives of Rice and Wilton was likely to be as difficult as those of the other three victims of these motiveless murders. There was nothing for it but another circular to Chief Constables, this time adding the Midlands. The dates, also, would be a little more explicit. There would be no need to waste time looking for them after 1909. Dewar was drafting the message when the local sergeant entered the office deferentially. It was only the third time in his career that he had met, officially, a real inspector from headquarters.

"I beg your pardon, sir," he said, "but there's one of these witnesses, though, of course, they're not strictly speaking witnesses, as you and I know, sir—he's remembered something he'd forgotten that he remembered—if you take my meaning, sir."

"I take it, Sergeant. Bring him in." The Sergeant returned with one of the nine, a sensible, elderly man, a carpenter by trade. "I've just remembered, sir, that two years ago or more another gentleman came asking about Rice and Wilton."

Only Dewar's long training and dour, Lowland upbringing prevented him from starting out of his chair with a shout. He simply said, "Yes?"

"I don't know if it's important, sir."

"Perhaps it is. What was the man like?"

"It was a very queer-looking man. I took particular notice of him because he was so queer-looking. He was a big man with black eyebrows and his face was the thinnest face I've ever seen. It was all hollows where it should have been bulges and it all seemed to be black. It wasn't black of course, but it looked as if it was. I don't know why. He was queer. Do you know what I thought, sir. I thought it was a lunatic, he looked at me so strangely."

"What did he want to know?"

"Just the sort of thing you asked, sir." The man stopped and then said, "No, I'm wrong there, sir. There was a difference. If you'll excuse me saying so, sir, you seemed to want to know where these men had come from. This other gentleman wanted to know where they had gone to."

"Do you remember anything else about him?"

The carpenter considered carefully and then shook his head.

"No, sir, I'm afraid not.

"About two years ago, you say?"

"Between two and three."

Dewar took out his pocket-book, extracted a photograph of Henry Maddock and handed it to the man.

"Was he anything like that?"

The carpenter looked at the photograph and answered promptly and decisively. "No, sir. They're both big and both got heavy eyebrows but there's no other likeness."

"None at all?"

"None, sir. I'm quite certain."

Dewar got up and held out his hand. "Thank you very much. I am greatly obliged to you." The Sergeant came forward and helped Dewar into his overcoat. "Going back to London, sir?" he asked. "I hope your visit has been profitable."

"It has been unexpectedly profitable," said Dewar with a suppressed gleam of excitement.

"The first bit of luck," he said to himself as he slipped into top gear and headed for London. "Some sort of a description of the murderer himself."

CHAPTER VIII

The Attack on Henry Maddock

Superintendent Bone was pleased with the results of Dewar's visit to Petworth. He rubbed his large red hands together and raised his voice considerably above its ordinarily gentle tone. "At last something tangible," he exclaimed. "To tell you the truth, Dewar my lad, in strictest confidence between ourselves, the folk upstairs," he jerked a podgy thumb in the supposed direction of the Chief Commissioner's office, two floors below, "the folk upstairs are getting a bit restive. They don't seem to mind much about that Oliver Maddock and they don't care a row of beans about the tramp. It's the killing of a financial magnate outside the Bank of England that riles them. I believe it wouldn't have mattered half so much if it had been outside Lloyd's or the Mansion House. It's the Bank that sticks in their throats. It's sacred, you know."

"Shall I go ahead, sir?" inquired the more stolid inspector. He did not understand why it made such a difference where Skinner had been shot, but he suspected that Bone was making a joke and he was determined not to be caught.

"Yes, go ahead, Dewar. Circulate the description to all stations and to the Press, and get the South and Midlands to report about Rice and Wilton prior to 1909. And by the way, Dewar."

"Sir."

"Sit down again and check my dates. Let us assume that your Petworth pal with the thin face was the victim of a gang which consisted of Rice, Wilton, Stuck-up Sam, Skinner and Maddock, some time before 1905."

"They're an ill-assorted crew, sir."

"They are. But don't interrupt, Dewar. Assume that the man goes down on a lifer and swears vengeance on his friends—you know, the Lyceum melodrama stuff."

"Or Monte Cristo," blurted out Dewar before he could stop himself.

"Cristo?" said Bone. "Montague Cristo. I don't remember him. What line was he on?"

"It's a book, sir. I beg your pardon."

"You and your books. Well, he comes out from his sentence in fifteen or sixteen years. Seventeen at the outside. That is to say, some time before 1922. He starts laying for Rice and Wilton but he doesn't reach Petworth until about 1926. How do you account for that gap?"

"Took him all that time to find him," hazarded Dewar.

"Don't be silly."

Dewar thought hard. "Perhaps he wanted enough time to elapse for him to get rid of as much of his identity as possible before starting again. He might have gone abroad and lain low for a few years."

"That's ingenious," conceded Bone. "And it's possible. But I doubt it. If a man has waited sixteen years for revenge I should think he wouldn't waste much time getting to work when the chance came."

"What's your idea, sir?"

"That the man hasn't been in a British prison at all. Some of these foreign countries give the most devilish sentences, you know. Thirty and forty years with mighty little off for good conduct. Look at the whole case, Dewar. It simply reeks of other countries. South Africa, Belgian Congo, Canada, Holland, Dutch East Indies, a German pistol. The roots of this thing are abroad. Of that I'm positive."

The telephone buzzed on the desk. "Answer it for me, Dewar," said Bone. "I'm too comfortable to move."

Dewar picked up the receiver and listened. It was the voice of the sergeant on duty. After half a minute Dewar replaced the instrument with the words, "All right, Spink," and turned to the semi-recumbent Bone. "There's a report in from Enfield, sir. Attempted murder of Henry Maddock. Man caught."

The Superintendent removed his feet from the chair on which they had been resting and gazed blandly at Dewar.

"Well, well. What a waste of brain work! All our intellectual efforts wasted and the murderer caught by a local p.c. Where's the man being held?"

"At Enfield, sir."

"Come on, then. We'll go to Enfield. I should like to ask the fellow what it was all about. Henry wasn't hurt, was he?"

"A knife in the forearm."

"A knife? Gone back to the knife, has he?" He struggled into a huge overcoat and led the way to the Embankment where a police car was always in readiness.

Dewar could not help remarking for the first mile or two of the journey down that the large pink forehead of the Superintendent was occasionally ribbed with long wrinkles as he frowned over some problem that was worrying him. At last he shook his head and murmured, "It's a great mistake to waste time and energy guessing at a riddle when you're going to get the answer for certain in an hour or so."

Dewar was surprised. "I didn't think there, was anything more to guess, sir."

Bone smiled benignly. "Perhaps not, Dewar. Anyway I'm not going to worry about it." He lit his pipe and began to discuss the peculiar disappearance of a well-known Aldersgate 'fence' during the previous week and the report that he had sailed for South America under an 'alias.' He discussed at great length and with amazing grasp of detail the world-flow of stolen diamonds and the gradual change in the main line of the traffic from the Rotterdam – New York route in favour of the London – Buenos Aires. "And you mark my words, young Dewar," he was saying as the car drew up outside the Enfield police station, "Aldersgate Aaron has gone to Buenos Aires in search of new markets which means that he's got more stuff than he can handle, which means fifty to one that he's got the Mayfield necklace. Well, well. We shall see."

He uncurled himself from the car and the two detectives entered the station. The local inspector was ready with the full story of the attack.

At about midday a man had approached the tradesmen's entrance at Greenlawns and stated that he was a travelling inspector of the Grantham and Chelmsford Lawn Mower Manufacturing Company and that he had come to overhaul Mr Maddock's machine. The maid, after conducting him to the shed in the garden where the gardening tools, rollers and lawn mowers were kept, returned to the house and informed Mr Maddock. The latter, who took a great interest in the upkeep of the tennis courts, seized a hat and went straight to the garden shed. The under-gardener who was busy tying up sweet peas, saw the scene at the shed. The inspector was bending over the big mower when the 'boss' approached. The 'boss' called out "Good morning, inspector," in that big, hearty voice of his. The other whipped round and went for him with a knife. There was a brief scuffle and then the stranger went down like a ninepin, leaving Henry Maddock standing over him, pistol in one hand and a knife cut across the other. The under-gardener picked up a rake and ran to the rescue of the 'boss.'

At this point in the story, Superintendent Bone gave a dry laugh and remarked, "It doesn't sound as if the boss needed much rescuing."

"You're right, sir," agreed the local inspector. "Mr Maddock is as tough a nut as ever I met."

"Has he a licence to keep firearms?" asked Dewar.

"Yes. All in order."

"Go on," said the Superintendent.

"There's not much more to tell, sir. The head gardener heard the scuffle and came running up and the three of them marched the man down here and charged him with attempted murder."

Bone fingered his chin thoughtfully and then turned to Dewar. "Am I dreaming or do I remember your telling me a story about Maddock throwing a man out of a window some years ago?"

"That's right, sir. He did."

"I wonder if it's the same man."

"It might be, sir," said the local inspector. "I remember the window throwing affair but I never saw the man. He was described as middle-size, bearded, about fifty years of age with a queer accent. This man's the same, roughly speaking, but without the beard."

"Maddock didn't charge him last time, did he?"

"No, sir. Nor did the man charge Maddock."

"But he charged him this time, quick," mused Bone. "Well, let's have a look at him, Inspector. Trot him out."

The inspector went out and returned in a moment with a constable and the prisoner.

The prisoner was a thick-set, deep-chested man of about fifty, with grizzled hair, pale blue eyes and an untidy long grey moustache. His complexion was a dark red and his hands were exceptionally large and hard. His height was about five feet ten or eleven. There was no look of sullenness or anger about his face. He was calm and confident and looked at each of the detectives with a quiet interest.

"Sit down," said the Superintendent and the man answered civilly, "Thank you."

For about half a minute Bone looked him over from head to foot. The man betrayed no uneasiness under the scrutiny and seemed to find a hidden amusement in surveying the Superintendent in return.

"What's your name?" asked the latter when his first scrutiny was completed.

"Find out," was the answer in easy, pleasant tones.

"Why did you go for Henry Maddock?"

"Find out."

"Did he ever throw you out of a window?"

The man grinned and shook his head.

"But you know who it was?"

"I do."

"Who was it?"

"Find out."

"Do you know the penalty for attempted murder?"

"No. And I never shall."

"Why not?"

"Wait and see."

Bone lowered his eyes and examined his boots carefully. Then he looked up again and asked. "How many years were you on the Breakwater?" It was a hit. The man started perceptibly and Bone laughed, almost crowed with delight. "Look at that, Dewar, my lad. That was a good shot. The man's got Breakwater stamped all over him. Outdoor complexion, big chest, enormous hands, South African accent and a murderous scoundrel. The combination's irresistible. Breakwater, of course. Come now, Mr Convict, you can save me a lot of time if you tell me the whole story."

"Why should I want to save you time?" The man had quite recovered himself.

"That's true enough. Why should you? When did you first meet Skinner?" The last question was shot out at the man. He never moved a muscle.

"Skinner? Never heard of him."

"Then why did you murder him?"

The prisoner wrinkled his brows. "What's this new idea? I haven't killed anyone for quite a while."

"When was the last time?"

"In the English War. What you call the Boer War—I was a trooper in our light horse."

"Tell me this, Mr Convict." Bone leant forward and tapped the man confidentially on the knee. "Why are you so certain that you won't be charged with attempted murder?" The man smiled.

"You won't tell me, of course. But it's obvious. When Maddock knows all that you know about him, he'll get frightened and won't give evidence or he'll commit perjury. And he'll square the under-gardener. That's the idea, isn't it?"

The gleam in the man's eyes showed that Bone was correct.

"Very well," said the Superintendent. "Make your mind easy about that. You won't be charged with attempted murder. You'll be held here until I've got sufficient evidence to put you in the dock on the charge of murdering Aloysius Skinner."

The man made a contemptuous movement of the head. "Cut out that bluff, Chief," he remarked. "I'm too old a bird to get scared by that kind of talk."

"And if I can't get evidence for that, I'll wait till I get you for shooting Oliver Maddock." This was Bone's second hit. The prisoner jumped up and pointed a huge finger at the Superintendent. "Oh no you don't," he cried. "None of your frame-ups for me. I wasn't in England when that guy was turned off."

"You'll have to prove that," said Bone.

"I'll prove it quick enough. I was on a Castle liner two days out of Cape Town when Oliver Maddock was shot."

"Bring me your file of *The Times*, please." The Superintendent turned to the constable. The file was brought and Dewar rapidly turned back to the shipping news two days before the date of Oliver Maddock's murder.

"What ship was it, Mr Convict?" asked Bone.

"The *Excelsior Castle*."

Bone looked at Dewar who nodded. The prisoner laughed and then there was a long silence.

Then Bone got up with a deep sigh and said to the local inspector. "All right. Take him away. Come on, Dewar. Let's go up to Greenlawns."

"Give my love to Harry," said the prisoner over his shoulder as he was led back to the cells.

CHAPTER IX

The Mysterious Peter Hendrick

The two police officers walked in silence to Greenlawns. The first thing they saw on entering the gate of the small front garden was a scene of activity. Maids were throwing open shutters, a couple of men were unscrewing a steel grille—rather like a portcullis on a hinge—which guarded the front door and two enormous Alsatian dogs were tearing ravenously at a huge plate of meat which lay on the small plot of grass. Henry Maddock himself, his left arm in a sling and his big, handsome face wreathed in smiles, was directing operations from the top of the steps.

Bone took in the scene in one brief pause and then marched up to the steps, Dewar following. "Hullo, Mr Policeman," shouted Maddock cheerily. "Glad to see you. Come in and have a drink. Bring your friend with you. Come round to the side door. This one isn't quite unbarred yet." He laughed loudly and sprang from the steps in one bound on to the gravel path, seized and shook the detectives by the hand and led the way round the house to a side door. A second steel grille was leaning against the wall beside it and Maddock gave it a hearty kick as he passed. "Capture of the besieging army, eh? Down with the fortifications. Come in."

He put the detectives into comfortable chairs, poured out two whiskies and sodas and opened a box of Corona-Coronas. "Now, gentlemen, I am at your disposal. Inspector what can I do for you?"

"This is my chief, Superintendent Bone," said Dewar.

"I am proud to meet you, sir. Tell me in what way I can serve you."

The Superintendent shot a quick glance at the handsome, triumphant, cruel face before him and then asked.

"Who was that man?"

"He was Peter Hendrick," was the prompt reply. "The cleverest, the most unscrupulous and the most treacherous of all the I.D.B.'s."

"Hm. I thought it was diamonds. But he got caught?"

"Yes. He overreached himself and got fifteen years on the Breakwater for it."

"Do you happen to remember the years he served?"

"Not off hand. But I should say 1912 to 1927.

"Now, tell me, Mr Maddock, why had he such reason to dislike you?"

"For marrying what he was pleased to regard as 'his girl.'"

"Was that the only reason?"

Maddock laughed. "To a man of Hendrick's type it was enough."

"But there was no other reason?"

"None." For the second time Dewar had the impression that Maddock's straight look was almost too straight to be true.

Bone mused aloud. "So he brooded over it for fifteen years on the Breakwater, came out, sailed straight for England and shot your brother."

"And then attacked me."

"True. And then attacked you with a knife. Doesn't it strike you as a very odd procedure?"

"What is odd?"

"Well, sir, consider. This man wants to kill you. So he first makes a most efficient job of shooting your brother with a long-range air-pistol as a sort of preliminary and then, when he comes to the real job, makes a horrible, and I may say, fortunate, bungle of it with a knife."

"Thank you, Superintendent, for the word fortunate," said Maddock with a smile. "I've got two theories to account for it, though I daresay they'll sound very amateurish to you professors."

"Let's hear them, sir," said Bone non-committally.

"Well, the first is that Hendrick brooded over the thing for so long that when he finally saw himself in a position to get back at me, he lost his head with excitement and simply blazed away at random."

"And the second?"

"The second is perhaps more subtle. He might have looked at it from this angle. 'If I shoot Maddock, it'll be fun for me to get back on him. But he won't know it was me who did it. That will detract considerably from the fun. Therefore I'll shoot his brother first as an indication of what's coming. That will give him a month or so in hell and then I'll kill him.'"

Maddock leaned back in his chair and surveyed the impassive faces of the two detectives.

"How about that?" he said to Dewar. Dewar looked as wise as he could and said nothing.

Bone nodded repeatedly and murmured, "Ingenious. Most ingenious."

"As for attacking me with a knife instead of a pistol there may be a dozen different reasons for that."

"I should like to see your under-gardener," said Bone irrelevantly and Maddock raised his heavy eyebrows.

"Certainly. I'll fetch him myself." Maddock went to the side door of the house and the detectives could hear his powerful voice shouting, "William. Come here a moment."

He returned with the under-gardener, a short middle-aged man who shuffled nervously into the room and eyed Bone and Dewar with alarm and uncertainty.

"Come in, my man," said the Superintendent reassuringly. "I just want to ask you one question. How far were you from Mr Maddock when this man attacked him?"

The under-gardener considered the question and then said huskily, "about twenty yards, sir."

"Thank you. That is all." The gardener looked at the three men in a puzzled way and then shuffled out again.

"And now the head-gardener, please," said Bone.

Again Maddock went out and yelled a name returning a moment later with the head gardener. This functionary was a very different type to his subordinate. He walked slowly and talked slowly. He was perfectly calm and at the same time respectful. There was a quiet, incurious look in his eyes as he surveyed the group in the room.

"You're John Harding?" asked Bone and the gardener answered, "I am, sir," in a strong country accent.

"Buckinghamshire, surely?"

"Yes, sir. I come from Marsh Gibbon, near Bichester."

"Have you been at Enfield long?"

"Seven year next Michaelmas."

"Thank you, Harding. That's all I wanted to know."

The gardener with a civil "Good morning, sir," retired.

"That was most mysterious," Maddock observed with a laugh. "I suppose I mustn't ask what it was all about."

The Superintendent paid no attention to this but fixed his eyes admiringly on Henry Maddock's great shoulders and chest. "You must have been a powerful fighter in your day, sir," he remarked. "Hendrick apparently went down like a ninepin and he's no chicken."

"I was a keen amateur boxer for years."

Bone went off on another track.

"Mr Maddock, what would you say if you were told that, on the day your brother was shot, Peter Hendrick was two days out of Cape Town on a Union Castle liner?"

Maddock smiled.

"What would I say? I think I should say 'Rats' or 'Fiddlesticks.'"

"You wouldn't believe it?"

"I most certainly would not."

"Is there any chance of your telling us where you were between the outbreak of the Boer War and 1905?"

Henry Maddock answered with such smooth promptitude that Dewar felt certain that he had been expecting the question.

"Certainly I'll tell you. Why not? I was in Belgian Congo."

"All the time?"

"All the time."

"And when did you leave Belgian Congo?"

"I think it was in 1907."

"Not earlier?"

"No. Possibly it was 1908."

"Those fortifications that you're taking down, Mr Maddock," proceeded Bone with another of his sudden changes of topic, "You're quite certain you won't want them any more?"

"I don't quite understand."

"I mean, do you think that Hendrick has any allies who will carry on his work?"

"I've only been married once, Superintendent. No one else that I know of has a grudge against me."

"Thank you, Mr Maddock. I think that's all I wanted to know. We won't take up any more of your valuable time. Come along, Dewar."

"Have another drink," urged their hospitable host, but Bone declined. "We've a lot of work to get through yet," he explained.

"Well, Dewar, what do you make of it all?" he asked as they walked back to the police station.

"It's rather difficult to form an opinion until we've checked Hendrick's statement," was the cautious reply.

"Have you noticed a funny thing about it all, Dewar, how everything that turns up is almost exactly what we want but not quite. I mean, we suspected a revengeful convict from a foreign or colonial prison. The exact fellow we suspect appears. But his sentence, according to Maddock, didn't expire until 1927, which rules him out from killing Rice and Wilton. Then Hendrick attacks Henry Maddock but says he can prove an alibi on the charge of killing Oliver. Then our vital date, the meeting of all these men's lives, is some time before 1905. Hendrick didn't go to prison till 1912 or thereabouts."

"He may have been in prison twice or more."

"That's true. But there's another point. When our murdering cutthroat appears he doesn't seem so very murderous. I can't believe that the deadly and ruthless efficiency that killed Skinner and the others was the same hand that scratched Henry Maddock on the forearm. Again, there's something very queer about Henry Maddock, don't you think?"

"Very queer," assented Dewar.

"We're not by any means at the end of the hunt yet," sighed Bone. All the walking was making him very hot. "I thought the taking of this Hendrick would finish it off. We'd better go and see him again."

The prisoner was again paraded for the headquarters officers.

"Back again, Peter," began Bone cheerfully and the man shrugged his shoulders.

"Oh, yes, we know a bit more about you now. Tell me, Hendrick, what do you think of Maddock's under-gardener?"

The effect of this question on the man astonished Inspector Dewar. His mouth fell open and his blue eyes were round and staring.

"Mynheer, you are a very clever man," he said at last in admiration and Bone beamed at the compliment. "I can see you know more than you pretend. I will tell you the true story. Henry Maddock and I and three others, whose names don't matter as they're all dead; joined in a partnership in 1907 for trading in diamonds. In 1911 Maddock accepted ten thousand pounds from one of the big Syndicates to denounce us to the police and turn King's Evidence. In 1912 on Maddock's evidence we got fifteen years on the Breakwater. The other three died. I came home to find Maddock."

"What for?" interjected Bone, but Hendrick smiled. "Find out. Anyway, it was easy to get on to his trail because of all the fuss about the murder of his brother. I was on the *Excelsior Castle* at the time, as I told you. I took a room in a hotel and came down here. I went in and said I was an inspector of lawn mowers. While I was looking at one of the machines, Maddock came out of the house. He had a gun in his hand and he looked like the devil. He asked me what I wanted. I said I wanted money for the families of our three dead partners. He pretended to think this over and then he called up the under-gardener. They went for me and knocked me out. When I came to, I found Maddock bleeding from a scratch from my knife; he did it himself. And they had their story ready for these gentlemen here."

"Why didn't you tell this before?"

"Because I knew Maddock wouldn't have the face to press the charge."

"But he is pressing it."

"That's because he's certain that he'll get me on the murder charge. But he won't. My alibi's cast-iron."

"I've known cast-iron alibis before that came unstuck," said Bone gently.

"This one won't," said Hendrick, confidently.

"All right," said Bone. "That will do for the present." As soon as he was alone with Dewar he went on briskly. "We'll get back to the Yard, and perhaps our friend the local inspector will make some discreet enquiries about that gardener. Speak to him about it, will you? Tell him not to let Maddock think we've got any reason to doubt his story. We must get on as quickly as we can with the verification of Hendrick's story. If it's all true, we're as far away from the end of this thing as ever."

CHAPTER X

A Fishy Household

The story related by Peter Hendrick was confirmed by the Cape Town police. Hendrick, George Hollis, Albert Stejnwijk and Jan Pieterson had been convicted of illicit diamond buying in 1912 and had been sentenced to fifteen years in prison. Hollis and Stejnwijk had died in prison and Pieterson had been shot dead by a warder in 1916 while trying to escape. Hendrick had been released in 1927. He had reported at the prescribed intervals up to April, 1928, when he disappeared. The steward in the steerage of the *Excelsior Castle* identified the Enfield prisoner as one of the men who had travelled in that liner on the voyage which began two days before the death of Oliver Maddock. In the meanwhile the headquarters of the Belgian police in Brussels telegraphed that Henry Maddock had spent three years in a Congo prison from 1900 to 1902 for the murder of a half-caste and two natives.

When these reports arrived, Dewar pulled out of his drawer the file of papers about the whole series of murders, in another painstaking and laborious effort to discover a ray of light in the business. He pored over every document, reading every word slowly and carefully, until he had finished the last telegram. Then he sat back in his chair and filled his pipe.

The truth was that the inspector was a little muddled. He was accustomed to seizing on a clue or on a definite line of investigation and pursuing it doggedly to the end. It was this capacity that had steadily advanced him in rank to his inspectorship. But in this case there were so many different lines to pursue and it was essential to keep them all in his head at the same time. At any moment a fact was likely to crop up which would make a connection with one of the facts already in his possession, but if he could not remember what facts actually were in his possession, he would probably miss some vital point.

He did his best, therefore, to memorise all the different angles of the investigation, and then he turned to the latest and freshest development. What part did Peter Hendrick play in the case and who was the man who shot Oliver Maddock, since Hendrick obviously did not? Presumably the murderer was an accomplice of Hendrick's. But the Cape Town police definitely stated that his accomplices died in prison. Suppose there was one who hadn't died in prison and suppose he came over and shot Oliver Maddock. That man would still be at large. Then why was Henry Maddock so confident that all the danger was over? Why had he so cheerfully demolished the fortifications of Greenlawns? Because he was quite certain that he was safe from the murderer of his brother. Then, concluded Dewar, Henry Maddock must know that the murderer was either in prison or dead. He was not in prison. Therefore Maddock knew he was dead. "Probably killed him and buried him in the garden with the help of that under-gardener," he reflected. "Maddock would be up to any-thing of that kind. I must tell old Bone about all this. And that reminds me, I've not had the report from Enfield about that gardener."

He called up the Enfield station and was told that the report was in the post. "Give me the gist of it, Inspector. I'm in rather a hurry," he said.

"There's not much to tell, Mr Dewar," said the Enfield inspector. "The man's a stranger to the locality. Mr Maddock brought him with him. He doesn't mix much with the folk here and when he does they don't like him. He's pretty familiar with Maddock by all accounts and he's always got money to chuck about. Drinks fairly heavily, whisky. We've never had any trouble with him, though. The head-gardener says he's no use in the garden. In fact the head-gardener hates him. He says he would never have stuck the job with an assistant like that if it hadn't been for the high wages and the difficulty of getting jobs in these days. The head-gardener's wife is ill and he'd swallow pretty nearly anything for money. That's about all."

"Thanks very much," said Dewar and rang off.

"It's a fishy household," he added to himself. "I'll go and see old Bone."

The Superintendent was deep in the examination of a blackmail case when Dewar knocked, but he put it aside at once on seeing his subordinate. "Come in, young Dewar," he said. "Your five murders are a good deal more important than a silly little Countess who has been fool enough to write to her second chauffeur. What's the news?"

Dewar sketched his theory that Oliver Maddock's murderer might be lying buried in one of the flower beds at Greenlawns. Bone rubbed the top of his head with the palm of his hand. "It's possible," he conceded. "It's undeniably possible. And I call it jolly ingenious, of you, my lad.

Dumbartonshire is looking up. But before we go ahead with a search warrant and a digging party, we must do a little more thinking. Let's consider Hendrick. He might have had another friend who didn't die on the Breakwater and who shot Oliver Maddock.

Did that man also appear in Petworth two and a half years ago and inquire about Rice and Wilton? And if so, what grudge did he and Hendrick have against those English sheepfarmers?"

The Superintendent did a thing that Dewar had never seen him do before or had ever heard of him doing. He heaved himself out of his chair and marched ponderously up and down the room, the floor trembling under his elephantine tread.

"This is a most infernal case, Dewar," he exclaimed. "Thirty-five years I've been in the C.I.D. and I can't remember one like it. I've known lots of murder cases where there weren't any clues and there was nothing to go on, but I've never known a case before where clues were hanging out in scores and not one of them led to anything. I'm half inclined to think that it's some infernal madman like Jack the Ripper who's doing it all. And yet I find it difficult to believe. The Maddock part of it makes me think it must be a case of revenge. Look at it. There you have the whole traditional paraphernalia of a revenge-melodrama. The rich man with the foul past, his friends betrayed to the Breakwater, the return of the survivor, and then—pouf—the utterly inexplicable mistake in killing the wrong man and the cast-iron alibi of the obvious murderer. It's like doing police work in a nightmare where everything is just sufficiently wrong and so nearly right as to make the brain reel." He stopped abruptly, sat down again as if slightly ashamed of his outburst and added mildly, "It's rather annoying, you know, Dewar. And the folk upstairs are getting very restive about it all. The Press are getting questions asked in the House about us."

"So I see," said Dewar. After a pause he went on, "Have you any suggestions for the next line of action, sir?"

Bone shook his head thoughtfully. "I don't think so. Let me see. There are two circulars out, aren't there?"

"Yes, sir. One asking for information about Rice and Wilton and the other with the description of the Petworth man."

"But apart from those we're pretty well at a dead end?"

"Except for Maddock's garden."

"Maddock's garden. Hm! I think we'd better leave that for a day or two."

There was a knock at the door and a sergeant entered.

"I've made that enquiry into the life sentences, sir," he said.

"Oh, yes. And the results?"

"There were seven men, sir, sentenced before 1905 who were not released until 1925 or later."

Bone sat up. "Seven? That's rather a lot, isn't it?"

"Yes, sir. It's very exceptional."

"What happened?"

"Extra sentence for attempted murder and prison breaking in both cases."

"Tell me about it."

"In December, 1914, four convicts at Princetown attempted to escape in a snowstorm. They were stopped by two warders whom they attacked with iron bars and left for dead. They were recaptured on the following morning and sentenced to ten years' penal servitude. Their names were Foster, Box, Fountain and Pearson, serving life sentences for murder, convictions dating from before 1905. They were released on different dates in 1926 and 1927."

"And the other three?"

"Similar case, sir. Attempted escape from Peterhead Gaol, Aberdeenshire. Three men attacked a warder and made off in a boat. Recaptured trying to land near Fraserburgh. Sentenced to seven years' penal servitude. Names, Anderson and Macwhite, serving life sentences for murder, and Harter, attempted murder, convictions dating from before 1905. They were released on different dates in 1925 and 1926."

"Is that your report there, Sergeant?"

"Yes, sir."

"Please hand it to the Inspector. That is all, Sergeant."

Dewar looked at the report and murmured the names of the unfortunate men.

"I'm certainly surprised to find as many as seven," pursued Bone. "To tell the truth, when I put the enquiry through to Records, I didn't think there would be a single name."

"Do you think any of these men—" began Dewar and the Superintendent interrupted.

"Frankly I don't. I think, as I've said before, that the roots of this thing are abroad. However, we must follow it up. Put a man on to getting the photographs and descriptions of these men as they were when they came out and send him down to Petworth to see your carpenter. Then you'd better go over the trials of these men yourself, Dewar. If one of them is the man we want you'll be more likely to spot the connecting links than if we turn the job over to Records. I don't think for a moment you'll find anything. But it will be something to tell the people upstairs." Dewar returned to his own office, sent up to the Records Department for the necessary documents and sat down to study them. At first sight they did not seem promising. Two of the men, Foster and Macwhite, had murdered their sweethearts in mad fits of jealousy; Pearson had murdered a girl for refusing to become his sweetheart; Fountain had killed a man in a street fight in a Sheffield slum and his plea of self-defence had secured the commutation of his sentence but not his acquittal; Harter had been sentenced to fourteen years for shooting, but not killing, a policeman when surprised in a burglary in the neighbourhood of Hatton Garden; Box had killed a young man whom he suspected of having seduced his wife and, lastly, Anderson had been caught in a Glasgow flat by its owner, had punched the owner on the jaw and escaped. The owner's head had struck the edge of the fender and he had died.

This was the humdrum catalogue of crime as revealed by the all-recording card index. Dewar turned to the dusty files containing the stories of the trials and read each account slowly, searching for the word, the phrase, the name, the occupation which would make a connection with Henry Maddock or the tramp or Aloysius Skinner or the shadowy Van Doone or the sheep farming emigrants or Peter Hendrick or the Colonial Development Company or the Breakwater or any other phase of the puzzle.

For two hours he read, without stopping, from the first word to the last of the seven trials. Then he sent to the Canteen for a plate of sandwiches and a large cup of black coffee and read them all through again. Finally he closed the seventh file for the second time. There was nothing, absolutely nothing, in any of the seven sordid tales that had the faintest connection with what he was looking for.

He reported the failure to Bone who shrugged his shoulders and said, "I'm not surprised. You've sent for the photographs and descriptions?"

"Yes, sir."

"You'd better send a man with them to Petworth, though it won't do much good. No word yet of Rice and Wilton?"

"No, sir."

"Wire the Petworth description to Alberta and ask if anyone can remember seeing a man like that."

"Yes, sir."

Bone pondered for another moment and then looked up with a smile, "We may have to dig Maddock's garden after all."

CHAPTER XI

The Body in the Herbaceous Border

More than a month had passed since a perfectly respectable guest at a perfectly respectable tennis-party in a London suburb had been shot dead in a deck-chair and nearly three months had passed since the murder in a taxi-cab of the Chairman of the Imperial Cochineal Company outside the Bank of England. The public, which had at first been thrilled, grew restive. The prospect, however faint, of being defrauded of a first-class, sensational murder trial was most disquieting, although the more usual way of expressing this genuine feeling of disappointment was to say "it's horrible to think of murderers like that being still at large." And now as week followed week and no one was arrested or even detained on a murder charge, public uneasiness became acute. The arrest of Hendrick seemed at first sight to be a real advance, but the ex-buyer of illicit diamonds proved his alibi up to the hilt and was committed for trial on the charge of attempted murder only. Public opinion was gravely disturbed by this new development. The ordinary man in the street could see at once through the trick which had misled the professional and, of course, somewhat narrow-minded and hide-bound, detectives; Hendrick was obviously the murderer and the alibi must have been an ingenious fake. But the police persisted in their delusion and people shook their heads.

Inspector Dewar had come to a standstill. A sergeant had taken the photographs of the seven convicts down to Petworth and had shown them to the carpenter. The latter had at once ruled out the man Harter as being too round in the face. He had swithered over the other six in amazed perplexity and had finally admitted that he couldn't say for certain. All six were thin, thin to a peculiar extent, with a dark and hard look about the eyes. The mysterious stranger had had just that look. The sergeant brought back his report to Dewar.

"Another wash-out, eh?" said the Inspector, after hearing of the carpenter's indecision. "But it looks as if we're on the right tack in one way. We want an ex-lifer. The carpenter's man has the same look as six ex-lifers. That's queer. Old Bone's first idea may be the best one. The man may be out of a foreign prison. Well, it doesn't take us any further."

When the sergeant had left him, he sighed heavily and gazed out of the window. Twelve weeks without an inch of real progress towards the murderer of Skinner, and the Assistant-Commissioner and the Commissioner himself "turning a little nasty about it."

It wasn't really very pleasant. Only old Bone didn't seem to worry. It would need a lot to worry old Bone.

He was wondering what his next move should be when a constable brought him a note from the Superintendent.

"Go and dig up Maddock. Take Wilkinson and four men. Warrant is waiting at Enfield. J. B., Supt."

Dewar was delighted at the double prospect of having something concrete to do and testing his own theory at the same time. He picked up Sergeant Wilkinson, an expert in soil and digging, the four men and a car. At Enfield he halted for the warrant and the Inspector and then drove to Greenlawns.

Henry Maddock once again received him, but his manner had changed. He was preoccupied and seemed anxious for the detectives to get their work over as soon as possible. He expressed no surprise at the warrant or at the prospect of having his garden dug up. He did not even ask what they expected to find.

"Help yourselves to drinks, Inspector, whenever you or your men want them. You'll find them on the sideboard. I know you'll excuse me if I don't remain with you during your work."

Dewar hastened to assure him that it would be quite unnecessary.

"I am at the moment extremely busy," went on Maddock, "and I may have to drive up to London before lunch. Ring if you want anything. You'll find spades and other tools in the tool-shed." He went out of the room, leaving Dewar in a state of perplexity. He had no warrant for the arrest of Maddock and yet he had come down for the express purpose of trying to find a dead body in his garden. The body, if it turned out to be there, presumably could only be the result of a murder by Maddock and the under-gardener. And now Maddock was preparing to go to London. Dewar made up his mind on the spot and followed Maddock into the small study.

The owner of Greenlawns was standing ankle-deep in papers, pulling out the drawers of a writing-desk. He frowned heavily on seeing the detective and then forced a smile.

"Anything more, Inspector?" he asked.

"I must ask you not to leave the house, sir, until we've finished our search."

After the briefest possible pause Maddock bowed slightly and replied, "Certainly. It's annoying as I had business in London. But I quite realize that the Law is the Law, and it's my duty to give you every possible assistance. You will find me in here when you want me."

"Thank you, sir," said Dewar, and he returned to his men who were already in the garden. He took aside one of the constables. "Roberts," he said urgently, "I don't want you out here. Go in and keep a watch on Maddock. He's in the study. Whatever you do, don't let him get away. But try not to let him spot what you're there for. See?"

The man nodded and slipped back into the house and Dewar went across the lawn to the tool-shed.

"Now then, Wilkinson," he said to his sergeant. "Get to it."

Sergeant Wilkinson was a specialist and, like all specialists, he had a slight contempt for all amateurs. When his services were not in request, he sat in a tiny room at Scotland Yard and read scientific treatises on geology and mineralogy. He was hardly ever sent out on a case. The cases always came to him. He was like a Harley Street expert. Very often he gave his opinion without leaving his tiny den. But occasionally he went out to give a practical demonstration of his skill. This was one of his practical demonstrations. He pulled out of his pockets two long coils of string and a packet of pegs. The three constables and the local inspector were given the strings to hold, one at each end of the two coils, and were then posted in pairs opposite each other along one of the walls of the garden so that the strings enclosed a strip of ground, a yard wide, running the whole length of the garden. Sergeant Wilkinson then walked slowly down the strip, hands clasped behind him and eyes bent on the ground. At the end, he moved the officers one pace sideways and repeated the performance. Sometimes he stopped and went down on his hands and knees and four times he drove one of the little pegs into the ground. When the whole garden had been covered, he made a careful examination of the flower-beds, and put two more pegs into a herbaceous border. Finally he walked across to where Dewar was seated on a garden-roller and said, "There you are, sir. Six possible places." Dewar jumped up, took a spade from the shed and walked eagerly across to the first peg. His theory was really going to be thoroughly tested. Sergeant Wilkinson seated himself on the vacant roller, lit his pipe and pulled a small German treatise on sub-soils out of his pocket. His work was over. He had no concern in the manual labour that followed, except to tell the labourers when to stop.

Dewar and his four colleagues worked away at the first peg for ten minutes and then Dewar shouted, "Wilkinson."

"Sir." The specialist put a forefinger in his book to mark the place and walked across to the diggers and peered into the hole they had made.

"No good, sir. Virgin soil." He went back to his perch on the roller and waited for the next call on his services.

The second, third and fourth pegs yielded no result and it was not until they had dug three feet below the fifth peg, in the herbaceous border, that they found the body.

The moment Dewar saw that the search was successful, he dropped his spade and turned sharply to the local inspector. "Inspector, will you take two men and detain the under-gardener. You'd better take all the men-servants. Draper, you come with me and we'll take Maddock. Quick now."

He led the way rapidly across the lawn to the house, entered by the side-door and went straight to the study. Henry Maddock was a dangerous man who habitually carried fire-arms and would have few scruples about using them. Dewar and Constable Draper never hesitated. Neither was armed, but they entered the study as if they were going to a tea-party.

Dewar halted on the threshold. Constable Roberts lay at full length on the floor with an ugly bruise on his forehead and there was a faint whiff of chloroform in the air. Henry Maddock had gone.

"Look after Roberts," snapped Dewar to his assistant and went across to the telephone. The instrument had been smashed to pieces. A poker lay on the floor beside it.

Dewar looked at his watch. They had spent almost two hours in the garden.

"Is he alive, Draper?" he asked anxiously. "Yes, sir. Pulse beating, sir."

"Good. I'll leave you with him. Get him to hospital or to the local station and report to me when you get back." He ran out into the garden and met one of the other constables running towards the house.

"There's not a soul about, sir," he panted. "I know. Where's the inspector?"

"Down in the basement, sir."

At that moment the local inspector came out of the kitchen-door. "All gone, sir," he cried.

"And I'm off, too," shouted Dewar. "I leave the place in your hands, Inspector. Detain anyone suspicious."

He raced out of the front gate of Greenlawns and sprinted down the road to the police-station. In less than five minutes he was speaking to Superintendent Bone and in less than a quarter of an hour an all-stations call had gone out to pull in Henry Maddock and his under-gardener.

CHAPTER XII

Poor Jan Hendrick

Inspector Dewar was immensely elated by the discovery in the garden at Greenlawns and his elation was not at all diminished by the escape of Maddock and the gardener. After all, that escape was a purely temporary affair. Maddock was far too conspicuous a figure to evade the police for long. There were plenty of photographs and fingerprints available and his capture was only a matter of days. The under-gardener might prove a slightly more difficult affair as he was of comparatively ordinary appearance. And in any case it might be rather a troublesome job to bring a charge home to him. No. The under-gardener did not really matter. Henry Maddock was the man. As for the body in the garden, it brought to an end, reflected Dewar as he motored back to London, the baffling series of murders and the annoyance of his superiors at the failure to trace the murderer of Skinner. And it was by his own logic that he had made the discovery. No wonder he was elated.

Superintendent Bone, also, was delighted when Dewar made his report. "You've done well, Dewar," he said. "The fault for letting them get away was mine for not giving you explicit orders, and I shall explain it to the folk upstairs. The truth is, young Dewar, that the laugh is on me. I didn't tell you to detain Maddock because I never thought you'd find anything. But you were fretting to try your theory so I thought it would be best to prove it wrong and take your mind off it. And now you go and prove it right, which is clever of you, though galling to my pride. But I shall tell the Commissioner about it. You'd better see it through yourself. Run along back to Enfield. Take the divisional surgeon with you and get started on the identification. Leave Maddock and his gardener to me."

Once again Dewar returned to Enfield and passed the time while the surgeon was making his examination in going through Maddock's papers. There was very little of interest. Dewar regretfully raked over a huge pile of ashes in the study fireplace. The fugitive had evidently felt that the blow was about to fall and had been preparing for several days to retreat. The documents that remained were mainly bills, receipts, acceptances of invitations to parties and a few purple or pink or green envelopes, highly scented and addressed in a flowing, feminine hand.

Dewar examined the whole house carefully and came to the conclusion that whatever documentary secrets it had contained had been centralized in the study. Henry Maddock was too old a bird to scatter incriminating papers all over the house. It was altogether an unsatisfactory search. The next step was to try and find the staff of cooks, housemaids, chauffeurs and footmen who had looked after Greenlawns and its numerous parties. Fortunately most of them had been local inhabitants and they readily came forward with such information as they possessed. It did not amount to much. A week previously they had all received a month's wages and notice to leave at once. They had liked Mr Maddock in a way, but they all admitted to a "queer sort of feeling" in his presence. Only one, the head-gardener, had any concrete information to give. He provided a detailed description of his subordinate. He had disliked the subordinate very much and had only stayed on at Greenlawns because the pay was so good. The under-gardener, in the first place, knew absolutely nothing about gardening; in the second he hardly ever did what he was told; in the third, he used to talk to the boss in a peculiarly guttural foreign language, and on the most familiar terms.

In fact, concluded the head-gardener epigrammatically, as a gardener he was only fit to push a roller and as a man only fit to swill a pint. The son and daughter had gone, it was believed, to Brighton and Dewar telegraphed to the Brighton police, asking that they should be traced if possible and watched. It was likely that the fugitive might communicate with his children. By the time that these enquiries had been concluded, the police-surgeon was ready with his report.

The body found in the herbaceous border at Greenlawns was that of a middle-aged man of between forty-five and fifty-five. He had been dead from eight to ten weeks. The surgeon could not make a closer estimate. The man had been bludgeoned over the head and the skull had been shattered by repeated blows. A diamond was tattooed on his right forearm and a dancing-girl in tights on the left. Two ribs had been broken and had set imperfectly, his right leg was withered as the result of a terrible wound received years before and the third finger was missing from his right hand. The rest of the surgeon's report was technical and Dewar read it over rapidly. Then he jotted down the main and obvious particulars and asked the sergeant on duty in the station whether he could see Peter Hendrick.

In a few minutes the South African was conducted into the room. He was as calm and tranquil as ever and surveyed Dewar with a steady eye. "Well, Hendrick," began the inspector. "How are you? Keeping well?"

"Very well, thank you," was the quiet answer. "Where is your fat friend?"

Dewar smiled involuntarily and then said, "You're on remand, aren't you?"

"Remanded for a week. Till tomorrow."

"You'll be released tomorrow, Hendrick." The South African was unmoved.

"Do you know why?"

"Yes. No evidence against me."

"Has someone told you about Maddock?"

"No. I've known all along that the swine would not dare to give evidence."

"Did you ever know a man who had a diamond tattooed on his left forearm?"

Hendrick's eyes narrowed and he paused before replying, "No."

"Or a man with a woman in tights on the right?"

"Scores of them."

"But never one with them both."

Again Hendrick hesitated and then he said suddenly in a husky, broken voice, very different from his usual confident tones, "For God's sake, Inspector, have you got the arms mixed?"

Dewar looked at his notes. "You're right, Hendrick. The diamond's on the right and the woman's on the left."

"And a withered leg?"

"Yes. Did you know him?"

"Yes."

"He's dead, Hendrick."

The South African muttered, "I knew it. I knew it." He straightened his shoulders and asked, with a forced return to his calm and quiet voice, "Can you tell me about it, Inspector. You see, I think it must be my brother."

He listened to the story of the search in the garden and the discovery of the body and at the end he said, "My brother had two ribs broken. Maddock threw him out of the window."

Dewar nodded. "So that was your brother, was it? I had heard the story. Tell me about him."

"He was younger than me, seven years younger," answered Hendrick, controlling his emotions with an obvious effort. "I wouldn't let him into the diamond-buying. It was too risky. But he was wild and he went off on his own. He traded guns from Angola to anyone who would buy them. It was profitable. Then Maddock heard about it and joined in the traffic. Finally there was the same story. It got too hot for them and Maddock gave them away. My brother escaped into Rhodesia and from there across into Somaliland. His friends were taken and his wife died of starvation or broken heart. He came back after the war, he was with Botha and Smuts during it, to find Maddock. He found him."

"It seems to me," said Dewar, "that you are lucky not to be where your brother is."

Hendrick nodded. "I guess it was that head gardener turning up that saved me. If he'd been out of the way they'd have done me in. As it was they had to fake up a story against me."

"Why did you carry a knife?"

"Force of habit. I've always carried one, though I've never used it. I've never had a use for it before."

"Before? Before what?" asked Dewar sharply.

"I've got a use for it now. That's all."

"What do you mean? What are you hinting at?"

But Hendrick only smiled and said dreamily, "Never mind about that."

Dewar saw that it would be useless to pursue the subject and returned instead to the dead man. "Can you give me some dates in your brother's life, birth and so on?"

"He was born near Pretoria in 1880, poor little Jan. He worked on my father's farm until the English war. We were together during the war. Afterwards I went to Johannesburg and he went back to the farm, or what was left of it. A charred ruin. But that was long ago. He came to Johannesburg in about 1906 or 1907. The farm was too quiet for a young chap. In 1911 the crash came and he had to run. I never saw him again."

"When did he come home to England to find Maddock?"

"I don't know for certain, but I should think it was 1926 or 1927."

"Why didn't he come immediately after the war?"

"He was shot in the leg in September, 1918, by one of Lettow-Vorbeck's snipers in East Africa. He was left for dead. Then he was picked up and spent four or five years in hospital. It was a terrible wound and it withered his leg. When he came out of hospital he was broke and couldn't get a job with enough money to save his passage home. It wasn't till 1926 that he managed it."

"How do you know all this?"

"There were ways of getting news on the Breakwater."

"If everything you say is true, Hendrick," said Dewar, thoughtfully, "you've no great cause to love Henry Maddock."

"No," was the simple answer, and Dewar was far more impressed than he would have been by a volley of threats and imprecations. "Do you know of any other people that your brother had a grudge against?"

"No. But I shouldn't be surprised to hear that there were a good many."

"But you know none of their names."

"No. I tell you I haven't seen Jan since 1911."

"Why did you take his death so calmly?"

Hendrick's eyes flashed for a second and then he said, "A man learns to take things calmly on the Breakwater. And I was certain Janny was dead. We had a rendezvous in London. He never came or wrote. Janny always kept his word."

There was nothing more that Dewar wanted to know which Peter Hendrick could tell. He shook hands with the South African and gave him a parting word of advice.

"Look here, Hendrick, you've made a pretty fair hash of things one way and another. Don't go and make it worse by doing anything silly. We want Maddock and we'll get him. If there's any killing to be done, let the Law do it and don't try and do it yourself."

But Hendrick only smiled and Dewar had to leave it at that. "Let's hope we catch him before Hendrick does, that's all," he said to himself. "Lord, what a devil Maddock is. He'll be best out of the way."

He returned to Headquarters and was told that Superintendent Bone wanted to see him.

He went straight to the Superintendent's room.

"Come in, Dewar," said Bone. "I want to see you. How's the identification going?"

"Finished, sir."

"Already? Quick work."

"It was a brother of Peter Hendrick. Jan Hendrick. He had a grudge against Maddock and came to England to find him."

"And what about Skinner and the others?"

"Peter says he wouldn't be surprised to hear that his brother had a grudge against a good many people."

"And he's been dead eight or ten weeks?"

"Yes."

"So the case is over, Dewar, eh?"

"When Harry Maddock's in the dock on a murder charge," was Dewar's rather grim response.

"Of course. But the brain-work is over, eh? The whole case is solved?"

"Yes, sir."

Bone looked up at the ceiling. "I expect you're right. But somehow—it's all so disjointed. It doesn't make what I call a nice, clean finish. It's all ragged and lots of ends are still sticking out."

"Maddock will clear all that up when we catch him," said Dewar confidently.

"All right. Run along," said the Superintendent, turning to a file of papers at his elbow.

CHAPTER XIII

The Disappearance of Henry Maddock

The pursuit of Henry Maddock came, at a very early period, up against the undeniable fact that a method of escape had been carefully organized and prepared. There were no traces of a hasty and clumsily devised flight. Everything had been thought out beforehand. Maddock was obviously the sort of man who left as little as possible to chance. He had not left Greenlawns in a motor-car. His own three cars were still in the garage and no one in the neighbourhood had seen a car drive up or leave the front of the house. The facilities for hiring a car at such short notice were comparatively small, being limited to half a dozen local garages; none of these had been asked to hire a car, nor had the telephone been used during the half-hour preceding its destruction with the poker.

Dewar was puzzled. It seemed absurd to suppose that Maddock had walked or run or even bicycled away. He must have known that the hue and cry would be after him at any moment and that his one chance was to get as far away as possible in the shortest possible time. There remained the only logical conclusion, that Maddock had escaped on a motor-bicycle; but here again there was a check. The head-gardener and two of the footmen positively declared that there never had been a motor-bicycle at Greenlawns and that if there had been they would certainly have seen it. A minute search of the sheds and outhouses revealed no trace of a motor-bicycle having been hidden away, and Dewar was puzzled. He sat down to think it out.

Maddock was a clever man; he would not do anything foolish, therefore he would not hit Constable Roberts over the head unless he was certain he could get away quick. That ruled out the possibility that he had run all the way to the railway station, a good ten minutes' run, on the chance of catching a train at the moment of arriving at the station. For he clearly could not afford to hang about the platform. Dewar looked up the trains and found that, in any case, there was no train that he could have caught without a wait of at least a quarter of an hour. Again, Maddock had not taken a car and had not hired a car. Finally, there had never been a motor-bicycle at Greenlawns.

Dewar jumped up. "He either vanished into thin air," he exclaimed aloud, "or else he had another place, quite close, where he hid a car or a bike." Taking a couple of men, the Inspector walked rapidly up the road and round the corner. It was a typical suburban road. The houses were all large, imposing and ugly, screened in front by laburnum trees and behind by gardens and orchards. It was unlikely that Maddock was the secret owner of one of these yellow-brick monsters. And yet, if Dewar's theory was right, the motor-vehicle for the escape must lie hidden very near to Greenlawns. Suddenly the Inspector saw a narrow lane, almost hidden by an overhanging lilac tree, which ran at right angles between two of the houses. He dived down it and came out, fifty yards down, on an open space. Building had been begun on it years before and then abandoned. A foundation of brick was overgrown with grass and dandelions and nettles. In one corner stood an old, dilapidated shed, of the sort in which builders lock up their tools, eat their meals and shelter from storms. The door was ajar and inside there was a strong smell of oil and petrol. The fresh tracks of a motor-bicycle and side-car were clearly visible on the earth.

Dewar was elated at the success of his deduction and eagerly searched the hut for traces of Maddock. But that careful gentleman had left nothing behind of the slightest value as a clue to his further proceedings, and Dewar returned to the Enfield police-station to send out a call for a motor-bicycle and side-car. Inquiries in the neighbourhood failed to bring forward anyone who had ever seen the inside of the derelict shed or the make of motor-bicycle and Dewar felt that he would only be wasting his time if he tried to trace the firm or individual who had sold the machine to Maddock. He therefore sat down with all the patience he could muster and waited for news. He had not long to wait. A powerful motor-bicycle and side-car was found early next morning lying in a ditch in the neighbourhood of Epping Forest and Inspector Dewar proceeded to the spot as quickly as he could.

If it was doubtful at first whether the abandoned machine really was the property of Henry Maddock a very short search turned doubt into certainty. For the bicycle had been left in a ditch beside a small country lane which ran along a particularly large and flat grass field. On the other side of the field stood an unmistakable aeroplane-shed and the damp grass showed up clearly the marks of an aeroplane track, running for about a hundred yards from the door of the shed into the middle of the field and there halting abruptly. Local farm labourers were easily found who had seen the aeroplane ascending on the previous afternoon and vanishing in an easterly direction, towards Lowestoft or Colchester.

The hangar was as devoid of clues as the bicycle shed had been or Greenlawns itself.

Dewar realized at once that there was nothing for it but another period of waiting, and, as it was likely to be a longer period than the last, he decided to fill in the time with an experiment. Returning to Enfield, he arrived just as the magistrate was discharging Peter Hendrick owing to the absence of evidence against him. Dewar determined to follow Hendrick, arguing that the South African was likely to pursue Maddock until the Crack of Doom and that it was possible that he knew of haunts and hiding-places to which the murderer might retreat. But Hendrick made no apparent attempt to pursue. On being discharged, he bowed to the magistrate without a word, slung his pack across his broad shoulders and walked at an even and quiet pace to the railway station. Dewar found him an easy quarry to keep in view as he never once looked round and hardly ever to right or left. He travelled to King's Cross and from there walked to a small hotel in the Euston Road and booked a room in the name of Smit. So far he had acted as Dewar had expected. It was his subsequent actions that surprised the Inspector. For the ex-convict from the Capetown Breakwater, the relentless avenger, settled down in his room and did nothing. He made no effort to continue the case and accomplish the mission which had brought him from South Africa and which would, presumably, be his chief, if not his only, object in life until it was fulfilled.

After the first day of astonishment, Dewar thought he began to understand; the only possible explanation was that Hendrick was as much in the dark about Maddock's whereabouts as he was, and did not know how to set about the search. On the other hand, Hendrick was obviously not the man to sit down in the Euston Road with folded hands to await divine inspiration. He must be expecting to get news of Maddock somehow and the only possible means was by information from a friend or through the newspapers. Dewar had taken the room exactly opposite the South African's, across a dark and dingy landing, and by cutting a small square peep-hole in the panel of his door was able to keep watch on his neighbour's movement. Not once during the whole of three days did Hendrick leave the hotel and not once were newspapers brought up to him. From this Dewar inferred that somewhere in England or abroad

Hendrick had a confederate who was searching for Maddock and would write or telegraph when he had found him.

On the third day a message was brought to Dewar from Scotland Yard that a light aeroplane, presumably Maddock's, had been picked up in the North Sea, some eight or nine miles from Harwich. This information puzzled Dewar considerably. He refused to believe that the presence of the aeroplane in the sea was due to an ordinary and simple accident and that the bodies of Maddock and the under-gardener were at the bottom of the sea. At the same time, although he was prepared to admit that Maddock had engineered his escape very skilfully, he found it difficult to think that he could have arranged for accomplices to pick him up at a given rendezvous in the North Sea, at such short notice and without using the telephone at Greenlawns. It was possible, of course, but unlikely, and there was an element of chance about such a proceeding that seemed out of harmony with Maddock's elaborate and skilful arrangements.

Nevertheless, the presence of the aeroplane in the sea must be due to accident or intention, and yet Dewar felt that neither was a really satisfactory solution. A telephone call to Brighton satisfied him that young Bill Maddock could not have been concerned; he was still at the Metropole Hotel, carefully watched.

The Continental police were keenly on the alert, but had nothing to report. Dewar, and Superintendent Bone agreed with him, was certain that Maddock had got away to the Continent, but he was quite unable to lay his hands on the craft, or on anyone who had seen the craft, which rescued the two men from the aeroplane late in the night of the day of the escape.

In the meanwhile Peter Hendrick did not stir from the hotel in the Euston Road.

CHAPTER XIV

The Hotel in Euston Road

Day followed day and still the ex-convict and illicit-diamond-buyer made no move. He apparently had no interest in life. He received neither letter nor telegram nor newspaper nor any communication from the outer world. On the other hand he did not seem to be hiding. For the policeman on beat in the road outside reported, in answer to a special question of Dewar's, that Hendrick would often stand at the window of his room for hours at a time, watching the endless flow of traffic below him. He made no attempt to conceal his face or his appearance, a fairly conclusive proof that he was not in hiding.

Dewar made two surreptitious entries into the South African's room during the occupant's brief visit to the bar of the hotel in search of tobacco and a bottle of whisky, but on each occasion he found nothing of the slightest suspicion or interest. The pack in which Hendrick carried his belongings was easily rummageable and Dewar swiftly rummaged through it. There was nothing in the room under lock and key and there were no papers of any kind. The air was thick with tobacco smoke and an old pack of cards lay beside a couple of empty whisky bottles on a chair. It was a thoroughly disappointing room to search and Dewar became more puzzled than ever. The pursuit of Maddock had by this time receded somewhat in importance. The finding of the aeroplane in the North Sea meant either that Maddock and the under-gardener were drowned or, a more likely alternative, that they had escaped to the Continent. Whichever it was, the responsibility for either their souls or their bodies had passed into other hands. The Inspector's interest and attention was almost entirely taken up by Hendrick. Dewar felt instinctively that mischief was on foot and that the silence and inactivity of the ex-convict was going to be the prelude for violence and sudden death. He himself would have been the last man to base any action whatsoever upon instinct. Dewar had the Lowland Scot's native distrust for instinct, impulse, intuition or any of the excuses that are put forward to cover irrational and illogical actions. He preferred to rely upon logic and reasoning and was under the impression that his conduct was never swayed by feminine and unreliable promptings. In this case, as in many others, the Inspector felt instinctively that something was wrong and then looked about for arguments to support the course of action that instinct had suggested to him. Arguments were not hard to find and they were mainly concentrated upon the character of Hendrick himself. The man was a self-confessed desperado, a long-term convict, a man with a terrible series of wrongs to avenge, a man whose life had been ruined and whose brother had been foully murdered. He had followed steadily upon the trail of Henry Maddock with a firm relentlessness and a tireless pertinacity until he had found him at Enfield. He had faced with calmness the prospects of being charged with attempted murder and the likelihood of a deportation sentence as the barest minimum. He had left the Enfield police station with serene self-confidence to pursue his quarry. And then he had sat down in a hotel in the Euston Road and done nothing more. It wasn't natural, protested Dewar to himself over and over again; it was absurd; it wasn't human; there was something fishy about it. And with these sentences echoing in his mind, he explained his own inactivity to Superintendent Bone and obtained permission to continue to watch the South African in the Euston Road.

The reports from the Continent were the usual crop of contradicting statements. The men had been seen in Brussels, had landed from a fishing smack at Cuxhaven, had taken passages and sailed on a Hamburg steamer to Rio de Janeiro, had parted company and gone, one to Amsterdam, the other to Naples, had not landed on the shores of France, Belgium, Holland or Germany, and so on. Suspicious boats had been sighted making for Bordeaux, Norway, Cherbourg and the Skager Rak. An unaccountable searchlight had been seen by a cargo boat near Ostend. A small aeroplane had passed over Lille, flying in the direction of Germany. But nothing came of any of these rumours.

It was on the sixth day of Dewar's hotel life that the message arrived from Scotland Yard which made the Inspector sit bolt upright and whistle. A parachute had been found in a field near Frinton-on-Sea, in Essex. Dewar slapped his leg in mingled annoyance and admiration, annoyance with himself at having been bluffed so easily into transferring the search for Maddock from Britain to the Continent and admiration at the murderer's foresight and courage in venturing on a parachute descent from an aeroplane at night. He must have climbed to a great height and then, on approaching the sea, have taken his courage in both hands and jumped while the aeroplane went on for a few unguided and erratic miles before it finally plunged into the sea. Dewar wondered if the under-gardener had also been provided with a parachute or whether Maddock had left him to his fate in the aeroplane.

What would Maddock's next move have been on alighting somewhere on the desolate coast of Essex, six nights before? The Inspector tried to think it out.

"There's one thing to go on," he said aloud. "Maddock had a plan of escape, organized down to the last hair. What did he do when he got down?"

Several points immediately suggested themselves. Maddock had deliberately drawn attention to his flight to the Continent by flying towards Harwich in daylight and by letting the aeroplane fall into the North Sea. Therefore he almost certainly did not intend to go that way. Secondly, it is impossible to gauge with any sort of accuracy where a parachute will descend. It depends on the variations of wind at different levels as well as on other more subtle and incalculable factors. Therefore Maddock had to be prepared for a landing at almost any part of the east of the County of Essex. He would have had to reckon with the possibility of landing eight or ten miles from the point at which he had stored, say, a motor-bicycle or motor-car, and eight or ten miles at night in a strange country might be a serious handicap to escaping murderers against whom the hue and cry is up. How then did Maddock make arrangements for getting away from Essex, arrangements that should be as nearly as possible proof against miscarriage? That was the problem.

Dewar went downstairs and telephoned to Scotland Yard, asking rather reluctantly that a man should be sent to relieve him in the hotel and that an inquiry should at once be started into the movements of cars, motor-bicycles and aeroplanes in Essex on the night of Maddock's escape. He then went down to Frinton to examine the parachute and see if he could find any indications of the method or direction of Maddock's subsequent movements. The Essex County Constabulary had already begun investigations but nothing of interest had transpired. The parachute had been found by a farm-labourer, hidden under a pile of brushwood in a ditch. A passage had been forced through a neighbouring hedge on to a country lane and there the six days' old trail came to an end. The ground was hard and retained no recent impressions of footmarks, nor was there any signs of motor-traffic. Dewar made a long and minute search of the field in which the parachute had been found but was not rewarded by any tangible result. There was one place where it seemed as if the man and the parachute might have first touched the ground but it was a problematical, and in any case useless, discovery. The Scotland Yard Inspector returned to Frinton and called for a map of the district. The spot where the parachute had been found was three miles from Frinton and about a mile and a half from the main road from Frinton to Colchester. The more Dewar pored over the map the more certain did he become that the key to the situation lay in Colchester. The town lies at the bottleneck of the Brightlingsea – Clacton – Walton – Harwich – Manningtree peninsula. Every road of any size or consequence in the peninsula runs straight to it, like the outspread fingers of a hand, from the sea-coast bathing places. If Maddock timed his fall so as to land in the peninsula it would be almost impossible to fall more than a mile or two from one or other of the Colchester roads. He would then, argued Dewar, walk to the nearest road, assume his most charming smile and beg a lift into Colchester from the first passing car. Once in the city he would either take a train back to London or the north, or, more probably, drive himself away in the car which he had previously installed in a convenient garage. If this reasoning was correct, it meant that the pursuit of Maddock had to begin all over again, six days behind. In six days a clever man might do much. Dewar frowned. It was an axiom at Scotland Yard that no man or woman whose identity was known could ever escape arrest permanently except by the somewhat too permanent method of death. Criminals had a chance of getting away so long as their identities were not known. Once the Yard knew whom it was looking for the game was up. But somehow Maddock was a little different. He was a man of immense experience of the byways and subways of life; he had an iron nerve, a cool brain and at least five or six years in which to plan his "get-away"; and lastly, he had plenty of money. Dewar wondered if he was going to be the exception that proved the Scotland Yard rule and make a permanent get-away. A shadow fell across the map over which he was poring. He looked up straight into the quietly pleasant eyes of Peter Hendrick.

CHAPTER XV

Frinton-on-Sea

Dewar sprang up as if a pin had been driven sharply into his person and gaped at the South African. At last he exclaimed, "What the devil are you doing here?"

Hendrick smiled gently and replied, "Taking the air, Captain."

"But how on earth—what the blazes—how did you find out?"

"Find out what, Captain?"

"Why, that——" Dewar stopped and glared at the man. "What have you found out?" he went on.

The other shrugged his shoulders and smiled again. This time the detective found his smile exceedingly annoying and he only kept his temper with difficulty.

"You're a funny fellow, Hendrick," he said, "Come and have a drink."

In the lounge of the hotel at which Dewar was staying the two men sat down in a quiet corner and Dewar ordered whiskies and cigars. By the time the cigars were lit he had decided on his plan of action.

"Now, Hendrick," he said, "I'm going to take you into my confidence. I don't ask you to do the same by me, but I'd be glad all the same if you would." He paused, but not a muscle of Hendrick's face moved.

"It isn't a coincidence that has brought you up here," he went on. "Somehow or other you've got wind of this parachute and the way Maddock was heading. I don't know how you did it but I'll say this: you must have a devilish smart friend about the place somewhere. The way he picked up the scent was downright smart."

Hendrick permitted himself the ghost of a smile.

"However, we'll leave that. It's beside the point. The point is that you're here. Now, just listen to me." Dewar rapidly described the progress of Maddock's flight up to date, the discovery of the parachute, and the deductions he had made which took him as far as the railway station, or a garage, in Colchester. At the end, he leant back, drained his glass and waited.

"Very interesting," said Hendrick finally and then there was a silence. Dewar ordered two more drinks and ventured on a direct question.

"Do you think Maddock would go back to Africa?"

Hendrick roused himself at the word "Africa" and answered, "Yes. But not to British Africa."

"Ah"

"Nor Belgian either. But Portuguese. Or a native state. Liberia would be a paradise for him."

"Ever been to Liberia?" put in Dewar.

"No."

"How do you think he'd try to get there?"

Hendrick shrugged his shoulders again. "How should I know? How should I know anything that you don't know, Captain?"

"You knew enough to come to Frinton, anyway," said Dewar rather moodily.

Hendrick allowed his smile to develop into a genuine grin. "Ah! But I've got that clever chum who finds things out for me," he said. "You mustn't forget him."

"I'd give a good deal to know how he heard about the parachute," returned Dewar; but the ex-convict refused to be drawn.

"I've put my cards on the table," said the inspector at last. "Do you feel disposed to put down one or two?"

Hendrick spread out his big, brown hands. "Cards, Captain? I haven't got a card in my fist, not even the deuce of clubs. I'd put them down if I had them, but they just aren't there."

"You know a lot about Maddock's past that might help. He's been in tight corners before. You know how he got out of them. He might use the same methods again."

"Tell me, Captain," said Hendrick, ignoring the appeal. "Why did Maddock choose this part of England for his escape?"

"There may be a dozen reasons."

"But only one that really counts."

"Why do you think that?"

"Because Maddock never does anything without thinking. If he chose this part he chose it because it was more suitable for his purpose than any other part. What was it more suitable for?"

"Yes, that's the point. Have you any ideas?"

"How could I have? I know nothing about the county of Essex, any more than I know of Siberia or the South Pole. What makes it suitable, Captain? That's what I am asking you?"

"Why not ask your clever friend?"

"My clever friend? No, that won't do."

"Then you won't help me?"

"I would if I could—perhaps," was the slow answer.

Dewar sprang to his feet impatiently. "All right. Don't if you don't want to. But don't forget what I said before, Hendrick. If there's to be any killing, let the Law do it."

But the South African's head had sunk on his chest and he was lost in thought. Dewar strode from the room, borrowed a motor-bicycle from the Frinton police and drove to Colchester.

His search of the garages of Colchester came to a quick and satisfactory conclusion. At the third garage which he visited he found exactly what he had been looking for. About six months before a big, broad shouldered man with a heavy black beard, giving the name of Norton, had brought an old American car to the garage and, explaining that he was going abroad on business, left it to be looked after. He had paid for three months in advance and at the expiration of that time he had sent a postal order to cover the next three months. Both on his first visit and in the letter accompanying the postal order he had impressed upon the manager the importance of keeping the car in a fit condition to be driven away almost at a moment's notice. It was to be kept full of petrol, oil and water, and the engine was to be started up every morning and run for ten minutes. The owner had called for it early on the morning after Maddock's flight, had paid a small outstanding bill and driven rapidly away. The car had stood so long in the garage that the manager was able to supply a very detailed description of it, down to the dents on the mudguard, the crack in the windscreen and the squeak of the near-side rear spring where the leaves of the spring had not been sufficiently greased. The description was circulated and Dewar returned to Frinton in time for dinner. Hendrick had taken a room in the same hotel but did not put in an appearance in the dining room.

Dewar's mind was occupied during his solitary meal with the minor but irritating problem of the South African and his arrival on the East Coast. The man's activity in the hotel in the Euston Road had been sufficiently puzzling and annoying. His amazingly swift and accurate news-service was even more bewildering and Dewar was gradually being forced to the unproved conclusion that the "clever friend" was really the man who had shot Oliver Maddock. The flaw in this argument was, of course, that there was absolutely no link of any kind between the unknown man and the murder, whereas Dewar was morally certain that the killer of Oliver Maddock was young Jan Hendrick, whose body they had found in the garden at Enfield. Peter Hendrick came back to the hotel at about eleven o'clock that night and passed Dewar in the hall with a quiet "Good Night, Captain."

Next morning, Dewar was aroused by a local policeman with a message. The old American car had been found six days earlier in a field near the town of Thetford in Norfolk. The inspector seized his bundle of maps and turned up Norfolk. Then he stared in amazement. Thetford did not seem to be on the direct route between Colchester and anywhere except King's Lynn. Yarmouth and Lowestoft lay away to the East, Cambridge and the Midlands to the West. Of all pointless places to escape to, Thetford seemed about the most pointless. It led nowhere except into the great cul-de-sac of Norfolk. It was a small town, in which strangers would be conspicuous and it was near no large industrial centre where hiding places are easy to find. The more Dewar looked at the map the more idiotic did Thetford appear. At last he struck the map with the palm of his hand and said aloud, "I refuse to believe it. It's as obvious a blind as I ever saw." He jumped out of bed, dressed and telephoned to the Thetford police station. Details about the car were meagre.

No one had seen the man or men who had abandoned it. They had left no traces either of their arrival in Thetford or of their departure.

"Doubled back to London," exclaimed Dewar, as he hung up the receiver, "and I'm going to double back too. I'm sick of this."

After breakfast he telephoned to Superintendent Bone and told him of his intention to return to Headquarters. The Superintendent concurred. The search had left East Anglia; London or the industrial north were the places to watch.

"The only thing I'm uneasy about," said Dewar, "is this chap Hendrick. He's got a source of inside information, dead straight from the stable. I don't like leaving him unwatched."

Bone considered and then said, "Look here, my lad, stay till this evening in Frinton and test it. You know and I know that Maddock and his gardener have left the East Coast. But does Hendrick know? According to your idea, he ought to find out some time today from this chum of his and if you're on hand you ought to be able to spot how the wink gets tipped. If nothing happens today, don't waste any more time on him; get the locals to watch him and come back."

With these instructions, Dewar went through the public rooms of the hotel in search of the South African and came on him emerging from the lift. He was wearing his hat and carrying a stick. On seeing Dewar he lifted his hat politely and murmured, "Morning, Captain."

"Going for a walk?" asked Dewar.

"No, Captain."

"Ah! Just going to sit in the sun?"

"No, Captain. I am going for a train journey."

Dewar just succeeded in avoiding a start of surprise while the thought raced through his mind, "The devil's going to Thetford."

"A long way?" he inquired as casually as he could.

Hendrick smiled indulgently. "Run along and play, Captain," and with that he strolled out of the front door and along the street.

At a discreet distance the inspector followed. Hendrick walked at an easy pace, stopping once or twice to enquire the way from casual passers-by, until he reached the railway station. Dewar was quite close behind him at the booking office, for he had never once looked round, and distinctly heard him ask for a ticket to Clacton-on-Sea.

Dewar looked back on that day at Clacton as one of the dullest he ever spent. For one thing Hendrick did everything so slowly. He walked slowly, he ate and drank slowly, he stayed so long in contemplation of the gay crowds on the beach that several times Dewar thought he had fallen asleep. In addition to the paralysing lethargy which seemed to have overtaken the man, there was the dogged persistence with which he gazed and gazed at merry-go-rounds and flying horses and swings and all the gilt and scarlet paraphernalia of the popular seaside resort.

Dewar propounded two theories to account for this singular day. Either the man was killing time once again, as he had in the Euston Road, and gazed at merry-go-rounds and flying horses in admiration simply because he had never seen such things before, or else Clacton was a rendezvous where he was to meet, and get news from, his mysterious friend. But, so far as Dewar could see, nothing occurred to prove the second of the two theories, and as the bored and disgusted inspector returned to Frinton he was forced to fall back on the first theory.

Outside the station at Frinton he ran straight into Hendrick who was waiting on the pavement. "What do you think of Clacton, Captain?" said the ex-convict.

CHAPTER XVI

A Denouement at Southend-on-Sea

It was not often that Dewar was so disconcerted that he could only gape, but this was one of the occasions. And as he gaped, he felt the same sense of irritation and annoyance that conversations and dealings with the South African always seemed to produce in his mind.

"What do you mean?" he snapped.

"I was only wondering if you enjoyed yourself at Clacton as much as I did," was the mild reply.

"What were you doing at Clacton?"

"I was giving you a holiday, Captain."

"What the blazes are you talking about?"

"Don't be angry, Captain. I thought you would like a day's rest from your duties so I went to Clacton. I knew you would follow me and that a quiet day would do you a world of good."

"So you knew I would follow you, eh?"

"I thought you were just as likely to follow me to Clacton as to the Euston Road."

Dewar turned on his heel with an exclamation of disgust and marched back in the direction of the hotel. After proceeding a couple of hundred yards he slackened his pace and immediately Hendrick slid quietly alongside him.

"Don't be angry, Captain," he said. "I am only trying to help you. I know where Maddock is."

Dewar halted and looked at him. "You know where Maddock is?"

"I don't know the exact spot but I shall in a day or two."

The man was so quietly confident that Dewar could not help being impressed.

"Where is he?"

"Ah!"

"How did you find out? I swear it wasn't that friend of yours who told you. I haven't taken my eyes off you all day."

Hendrick shook with silent laughter. "That invaluable friend of mine! No, it wasn't him. I'll tell you something about him, Captain. He doesn't exist."

"Don't try that stuff on me," said Dewar. "I wasn't born yesterday."

"He doesn't exist. I found my way here by a much simpler method. I don't mind telling you what it is now, because my task is nearly over." He spoke the last words in a low voice and there was smouldering fire in his eyes.

"When I left Enfield I hadn't the slightest idea how to find Maddock. I didn't know the country, the people, the customs, anything. But, I said to myself, the police captain will think that I know where Maddock is. He will follow me in the hopes of my leading him to the hiding place. My only chance is to follow the police captain. So when you took the room opposite mine" — Dewar swore shortly— "in that hotel I knew I had only to wait until you got news. You burgled my room twice, but I was expecting you. I burgled yours every day and you were not expecting me. So I found papers, messages; one in particular about the parachute at Frinton. As soon as you got it you left the hotel. I also left the hotel. As for my brilliant friend, he vanishes into the air. He only existed in the brain of a police captain."

Dewar could see that he was being laughed at, but he determined to ignore the banter and take hold of the essential point.

"And you know where Maddock is?"

"Yes."

"How?"

"It wasn't you this time, Captain. It was a thing I remembered hearing about him years ago. He once was in a tight place and lots of people were looking for him, combing the Transvaal for him with toothpicks. But he lay low for a month and then got clear away."

"What's that got to do with it? It's fifty to one against his using the same method."

"No, it isn't. The conditions are the same and the district's the same."

Dewar tried to make his voice sound casual and careless as he threw in the question, "What makes the district the same?"

But Hendrick was on his guard and smiled.

"Ah! You'd like to know that, wouldn't you? If you knew that you'd soon guess the rest. When I came down here, I said to myself, 'what is there about this place that made Henry Maddock choose it?' and as soon as I found out what sort of a place it is, I remembered that old story of his get-away in Africa."

They had reached the door of the hotel and suddenly Hendrick's quiet, ironic, bland mask fell off his face for a moment and he looked like a wild and dangerous animal. "Two days more, or three, Captain," he muttered in a harsh growl, "Two days or three and some old scores will be paid."

"Don't be a fool," began Dewar, but the other interrupted him.

"Do you think I'm going to let myself be cheated by a judge and jury. They killed my brother. I'm not going to let my work be done by the public executioner." He swung round and entered the hotel.

Dewar almost ran to the Frinton police station where he arranged for four plainclothes men to be detailed to watch Hendrick night and day. The inspector impressed upon them the urgency of the case. It was not only a matter of preventing a double murder but also at the same time of effecting the arrest of Maddock and the under-gardener. Dewar had not the slightest doubt that Hendrick had spoken the truth when he said he could lay his hand on Maddock within the next two or three days and it seemed obvious that he would waste as little time as possible in running down his quarry; there was always the danger that Maddock would pack up and move to another hiding place.

Dewar retired to his room and tried to puzzle out what the characteristics of the Frinton district could be that had so quickly evoked the all-important memory in Hendrick's mind. Then he remembered that Maddock had, beyond any reasonable doubt, left the district and moved as far north as Thetford. Had he returned? Or had he doubled back to London? Or had he gone further north to Liverpool or Glasgow? Hendrick was the clue that would solve all these riddles.

But on the next morning the unaccountable ex-convict had resumed his inscrutable mask and, to the intense bafflement and boredom of Dewar and the two local plainclothes men who took the day spell of duty, he spent the entire day at Walton-on-the-Naze, performing the same slow round of strolling and lounging that had so exasperated Dewar at Clacton. Anything less like the swift, cruel pounce of the avenger could hardly be imagined. Instead of a hawk, it was a loafer. Dewar's one consolation was the thought that the more time Hendrick wasted in his puerile attempts to annoy him, the quicker the end would come when the ex-convict settled down to business, and he was fully convinced that the day at Walton would be the end of the laborious practical joke. But he was wrong, for on the next day the same wearisome ceremony was performed at Clacton again and, on the day after, at Southend. But at

Southend the day was different to the others in this respect, that an incident occurred.

Hendrick was sauntering slowly along a stretch of esplanade, the three bored detectives following at an interval of about seventy or eighty yards. The South African paused for a moment to buy a box of matches from a penny-in-the-slot machine, then joined a small throng that was watching a Punch and Judy Show, wandered away from it with a yawn and sat down to watch a band of nigger-minstrels who were performing on the sands. He gazed at them with lack-lustre eyes, rose and moved slowly on to a seat where the air was less troubled by the twanging of stringed instruments and the crooning of Mississippi airs. He sat down and tilted his hat over his eyes and folded his arms. In a minute he seemed to be asleep. But it is impossible to remain undisturbed for long at a democratic seaside resort in the height of summer. A couple of darkie songsters came along the sands from the other direction, took up a "pitch" almost opposite him and tuned up. It was then that the incident occurred. Peter Hendrick suddenly tipped his hat back and shouted loudly, "Got you at last, Maddock." Then he jerked out a pistol and shot the two minstrels. Dewar sprang up and rushed towards him. As he approached Hendrick faced him with a smile.

"Good-bye, Captain," he said, and shot himself through the forehead.

CHAPTER XVII

Number Nine at Reading

"They're all dead," said Inspector Dewar to Superintendent Bone. "Peter Hendrick made no mistake. Two clean shots at about ten yards and then one for himself."

"He was a man who had suffered much," murmured Bone.

"He was, sir. If ever a man got what he deserved, it was Maddock."

"When you say 'Peter Hendrick made no mistake,'" mused the Superintendent, "what exactly did you mean when you emphasized his Christian name?"

"As a contrast to his brother, sir, who certainly did make a mistake when he shot Oliver Maddock."

"'Certainly,' is a strong word. However, we'll let it pass. And so the case is over."

"Yes, sir, as far as we shall ever know it. Now that both the Hendrick brothers are dead, I don't suppose we shall ever know just how Skinner came into it or why they killed that tramp. Funny thing, sir, isn't it, coming to the end of a case without any of the intermediate stages. But then it's been a funny case all through."

"But it's over now, eh?"

There was something in the Superintendent's voice that made Dewar hesitate before replying, "I never saw a case that was so completely over. Everyone connected with it seems to be dead."

Bone picked up a telegram which lay on his table and read it out. "A man named Cullen, a small chemist, was shot dead last night in his shop at Reading. A piece of white cardboard marked 'Nine' was found on the counter." Inspector Dewar looked at Superintendent Bone and Superintendent Bone looked at Inspector Dewar.

"I don't believe it," said the Inspector at last. "Oh, I say," protested Bone. "It's rank insubordination to disbelieve the statement of a superior officer."

"I didn't mean that, sir," replied Dewar in some confusion. "I mean that I don't believe it's got any connection whatsoever with these other murders. It can't have. Jan Hendrick did the other ones and he's been dead for eight or ten weeks."

"What about the cardboard?"

"An obvious blind. He's heard about the other bits of cardboard."

"How? It's never been published."

Dewar felt his exasperation rising. "It hasn't been published but lots of people know about it and people talk. And, in any case, why Nine? If it was the same man it would be number Six."

"The intermediate numbers may turn up in Patagonia or Timbuktoo," said Bone maliciously.

"There wouldn't be time for that. There was time for the Canadian murders because they were the first of the series. But there wouldn't be time for a man to kill Oliver Maddock, go to Patagonia and Timbuktoo to kill six, seven and eight and be back in time to do Nine last night at Reading."

Bone sighed. "You're a literal Scotsman, Dewar. It needn't have been Patagonia. It might have been Vienna. You can fly to Vienna in a day. Or Constantinople or Cairo."

"I don't believe it's the same series," said Dewar doggedly.

"You wouldn't like to go down to Reading and make sure?"

"I'll go if you like, sir. I could do with a day's holiday."

"I say, Dewar," said Bone thoughtfully. "Was Jan Hendrick anything like the Petworth man?"

"The Petworth man may have had nothing to do with it."

"True. You couldn't get any connection between Jan Hendrick and Skinner?"

"No."

"Nor between Jan Hendrick and the tramp?"

"No."

"Nor between——"

"Look here, sir," interrupted Dewar. "We worked it out that the only possible way to account for Henry Maddock's peculiar behaviour was that he had the body of Oliver's murderer buried in his garden. We dig up the garden and there it is. I don't see you want to look any further than that."

"I know, Dewar. It seems irresistible. But I'm not easy about it. There are so many things to be explained."

"I've got the murderer. That's all I want."

"We've never discovered why the man shot the wrong Maddock."

If Bone had not been his superior officer, Dewar would have sighed ironically. As it was, he merely said, "And as the man's dead, we shall probably never know."

Bone looked up at the Inspector with a comical smile on his large face.

"I'll make a bargain with you, my lad," he said. "You stay here and have a look at the Clerkenwell arson case. Young Cotton seems to be out of his depth over it. In the meanwhile, Henderson shall go to Reading with his microscope. If the bullet that killed the chemist is scored in the same way as the bullets that killed Skinner and Maddock, then you'll apologise to the shade of Jan Hendrick; say you're sorry to me and take the next train to Reading. If it isn't scored I won't worry you until——"

"Until what, sir?"

"Until murder number Ten comes along."

Dewar laughed. "Done with you, sir."

"All right. Send up Henderson to me and go and see Cotton. He'll show you the file. I looked at it this morning. The thing seemed to me to hinge on the ownership of the tinder lighter they found in the ashbin. But you'll see for yourself."

Dewar spent the day in the neighbourhood of Clerkenwell and it was not until past seven o'clock that he returned to his office. On his table lay an envelope addressed to himself in the Superintendent's sprawling handwriting. He opened it and shook out a small piece of cardboard.

Inspector Dewar seldom swore. Years of self-control had almost eradicated the need for an occasional outlet in profanity. But on picking up the cardboard he could not control himself. "Damnation!" he exclaimed loudly.

It was a third-class single ticket to Reading.

CHAPTER XVIII

The Mystery of Albert Cullen

By the time that the evening express had arrived at Reading, Inspector Dewar had completely recovered his equanimity and had made up his mind on the subject of his new investigation. At first, when the fit of annoyance was still lingering, he had determined to prove that there was no connection between the murders and to stick to the theory that the discovery of the body of Jan Hendrick had closed the inquiry into the deaths of Skinner and Oliver Maddock. But as the Great Western express whirled through Slough and Maidenhead, his Scottish commonsense reasserted itself and he realized that to approach this new case with a biased and prejudiced mind would be a grossly unprofessional act. By the time he had descended on to the Reading platform and was shaking hands with an old friend, Inspector Avory of the Reading police, he was ready to approach the problem of the murdered chemist with an open mind. And if his triumph of reasoning was overthrown, and Jan Hendrick turned out not to be the murderer, at all events he would have the consolation of chasing a live man and not a dead one, with the additional kudos to be gained from a successful charge at the Old Bailey.

Inspector Avory asked if he would prefer to go straight to the scene of the murder, but Dewar decided to drive first to the police station and learn all the available details before actually beginning his investigation. At the station he found Sergeant Henderson, the Scotland Yard microscope expert, preparing to depart for London.

"There's no doubt about the bullet, is there, Henderson?"

"There's always a possibility," began the expert cautiously, but Dewar interrupted.

"I know, I know. But as man to man."

"It's the same pistol, sir, beyond any reasonable doubt," said Henderson.

"Thank you," answered Dewar. "You're just off?"

"Yes, sir. No time to waste. There's a big bloodstains case come in from Huddersfield, and I'll be up all night. Good-night, sir."

"Good-night," Dewar replied absently. His mind was running on the possibility of Jan Hendrick being one of a number of avengers who all used the same pistol. Then he went into Inspector Avory's office, sat down and listened to the story of the murder of the chemist.

"The chemist's name," began Avory, "is, or rather was, Albert Cullen. He was a well-known resident in Reading and popular among his friends and acquaintants. He was not a rich man, but he had worked hard all his life and was fairly well-to-do. Comfortable, I mean, in a smallish way."

"Three or four hundred a year?"

"That sort of thing. Perhaps a little more. He had an assistant in the shop, a young fellow called Arthur Broad. It was Broad who found the body."

"Cullen a bachelor?"

"A widower. Three children, all married."

"All married?" Dewar's eyebrows went up. "What sort of age was Cullen?"

"Cullen was sixty-seven. His wife died in 1922 and since then he lived alone over the shop."

"I see," said Dewar thoughtfully. "He was sixty-seven. Go on."

"Living over the shop," continued Avory, "he reversed the usual procedure of businesses. The assistant went home at half-past seven, and the boss put up the shutters with his own hands at eight o'clock and locked the premises. It's usually the other way about. Last night Broad went off at the stroke of half-past seven. He's a keen Territorial, a sergeant in our local Terrier engineers, and he had a parade at a quarter to eight. He reached the drill-hall on his motor-bicycle at 7.40 and was in his uniform and answering the roll-call at 7.45."

"Quick work."

"He's a smart lad by all accounts. He was on parade until ten, gossiping and drinking beer in the sergeants' mess until nearly eleven and reached his home on the other side of the town at a few minutes after eleven. His father and mother were still up. He went straight to bed and his mother called him for breakfast at seven next morning. At three minutes to eight he arrived at Cullen's shop, unlocked the door and went in. Cullen was lying across the counter. Broad didn't take long to realize what was wrong and he went straight to the nearest doctor and then to us on his motor-bicycle."

"He always unlocked the door in the mornings?"

"Yes. He had a key,"

"A Yale lock?"

"Yes. The doctor says that Cullen had been dead for some hours for certain and possibly for ten or twelve. Two pistol bullets."

"Cartridge cases lying about?"

"No. And no smoke-blackening, though the whole shop isn't more than ten feet across."

"Was Cullen seen after seven-thirty the night before?"

"Yes. A Mrs Barney went in for a dose of ammoniated quinine at about ten minutes to eight. Cullen made it up for her and she drank it and chatted for a minute or two. Then she went out and a few minutes afterwards she passed down the road again and saw that the shutters were up. She remembers that distinctly because she congratulated herself on having been in time and not having had to trouble Cullen to come down and open the shop again. The people opposite actually saw Cullen putting up the shutters."

"Then I take it that someone came later, rang the night-bell and was admitted by Cullen; that he went in and asked for medicine, pulled his gun, shot the chemist and walked out again. The Yale lock, of course, shut behind him." The Reading inspector agreed. "That's what I thought. The only question is who was it?"

Dewar smiled rather grimly and said, "Let me give you a sketch of Cullen's life and character."

Avory stared. "I was just going to give you a sketch," he said. "Do you know anything about him?"

"I'll make a guess," answered Dewar. "I should say that Albert Cullen was a nice, amiable old boy who had any amount of friends and not an enemy in the world. He had lived in Reading ever since 1906, but no one knows anything about him before that. He was very, very respectable, never drank or smoked or betted or speculated in shares. He never talked about his past life and never mentioned that he had been in South Africa. He was a pillar of the Methodist Church, was scrupulously honest and universally trusted. There is not the slightest suspicion of a motive why anyone should want to murder him. How about that for a bird's eye view of the late Albert Cullen?"

Inspector Avory was surprised at the bitterness in the tone of the London detective, but he politely refrained from comment. "Not at all bad," he replied thoughtfully. "In fact you're right in everything except about two or three details."

"I thought so," said Dewar gloomily.

"Mr Cullen was a Unitarian, not a Methodist, and he lived in Reading all his life as his father and grandfather did before him."

Dewar stared at Avory and his jaw dropped. "Say that again," he said slowly, and Avory repeated, "Albert Cullen lived in Reading all his life as his father and grandfather did before him." He was really astonished now at the behaviour of the Scotland Yard man. Dewar struck the office-table a resounding blow with his clenched fist and said between his teeth, "I absolutely and emphatically refuse to believe it. It's utterly impossible. There must be a mistake."

Avory shook his head, but Dewar pounced on him before he could speak, "It's no good your shaking your head like that. You can shake it till you're blue in the face if you like. But I tell you, Avory, that this man Cullen was in Africa at some period between 1900 and 1906. He must have been. He was. I know he was. And that's flat."

The Reading detective was becoming a little amused at the vehemence and emphasis of this remarkable assertion and Dewar instantly cooled. "You must think I'm talking through my hat," he remarked with a smile, "but just listen to this."

He ran briefly through the sequence of events from the murder of the tramp onwards.

Avory was astounded. "So that was why Scotland Yard was so anxious to send a man down at once. We couldn't understand it. And I see what you mean about Cullen's past."

"If Cullen can be proved beyond doubt to have lived all his life in Reading," declared Dewar, "then the whole thing becomes a perfect nightmare. In all these cases there has been the one connecting link— they were all men whose lives are untraceable beyond 1905. If Cullen was a respectable little chemist here between 1900 and 1906 it knocks everything endways and the case becomes chaos. It's confoundedly nearly chaos already."

He got up. "There are three lines to follow. First we must go into Cullen's life inch by inch. Secondly, we must circulate the description of the Petworth man throughout the town. And thirdly we must circulate enquiries for stray South Africans."

"If you wait two minutes," answered Avory, "I'll put the last two in motion and then we might go down to Cullen's and see the shop and find out if any of his children have arrived yet. There are two sons, both in South Wales, tinplate industry, and a daughter who married a Bradford man. It was hard luck on old Cullen that none of them stayed at home, but the two boys got fine jobs and he couldn't ask the girl's man to chuck his. So he was left alone."

They walked down to the small shop and pushed their way through the crowd of bystanders who were gaping at the shuttered building. Inside, the gas was burning and Dewar's eyes became gradually accustomed to the artificial light. He made a swift survey of the interior of the shop, more from long-ingrained habit than from any expectation of finding clues that Inspector Avory had missed. Indeed he was not greatly interested in the crime and the method by which it had been committed. The antecedents of the victim were the objects of his whole attention. The shop had not been disturbed since the crime except that the body had been removed.

Dewar went upstairs and entered the dead man's sitting-room. There was a cupboard full of pharmaceutical works of reference and a writing-desk, each pigeon-hole of which was filled with neatly-tied packets of papers. This was what Dewar wanted. He took off his coat and sat down in his shirt-sleeves at the desk. An hour and a half later he lay back, stared at the ceiling and blinked. There was not a single document in the desk that threw the slightest ray of light on the affair. He got up and carefully searched, the rest of the house. Mr Cullen had evidently been a man of method. Every scrap of paper in the house was in the writing-desk. There was not even an old envelope, a faded prescription, a bill or a receipt anywhere else. He had just finished when he heard voices on the stairs and the next moment Avory entered the sitting-room, followed by two tall, good-looking men, a girl dressed in black and a somewhat older man.

"This is Inspector Dewar of Scotland Yard, Mr Cullen," began Avory. "Dewar, this is
Mr Cullen, Mr George Cullen and Mr and Mrs Newton. Mrs Newton is a daughter of the late Mr Cullen."

Dewar bowed to the party comprehensively and addressed himself to the elder son. "May I offer you my sincere sympathy, sir, on your bereavement?"

The elder of the two men answered quietly, "Thank you, Inspector. Are there any questions you would like to ask us?"

Dewar and Avory fetched chairs for the party and then Dewar began.

"There are only three questions I want to ask, sir. Had your father any enemies?" Cullen shook his head emphatically and the younger brother muttered, "Not an enemy in the world."

"Thank you. The second question is: who benefits by his will?"

"We three, equally."

"The third is; where was your father during the years from 1900 to 1906?"

"In Reading."

"You are sure?"

The elder son knitted his brows. "Let me work it out. I was born in eighty-eight so that in 1900 I was twelve and in 1906 I was eighteen. Nellie was born in 1899, weren't you, Nellie?" The girl nodded.

"And I know Father was at home from the time Nellie was born till 1902, and from 1902 I was taken into the shop and worked with him downstairs till 1908, and he never left Reading all that time. No, sir, I can state positively that my father was in Reading all the time between 1900 and 1905."

"Had your father ever been abroad?"

"I have often heard him say that he had never been further from Reading than Lyme Regis. It was one of his little jokes."

"He was born here, I understand?"

"Yes. My grandfather came here when he was quite a young man, before Father was born, and the family has been here ever since. It must be about eighty years now since grandfather came here. He was an Ipswich man.

Dewar held out his hand. "Thank you, sir. Those are all the questions I wanted to ask." The elder Cullen shook the detective's hand and said, "I expect it's unprofessional to ask, but do you see any light in this horrible tragedy?"

"Not yet, sir," responded Dewar gravely, and when the family had departed, he added bitterly to himself, "Any light? What little there was has gone. I never knew such a muddle,"

CHAPTER XIX

Uncovering the Quiet Past of Oliver Maddock

There was very little more to do at Reading. Ample confirmation was obtainable of the elder Cullen's statement that his father had never been out of England. A dozen old friends and cronies came forward and professed to remember clearly the years between 1900 and 1906. They also united in declaring that Albert Cullen had never hurt a fly in his whole life and that he wouldn't have known how to hurt a fly if he had wanted to.

It was impossible to find anyone who had seen the deadly stranger entering or leaving the chemist's shop, but a man came forward to say that on the evening of the murder he had seen a big car standing at the end of the street in which the shop was situated. But the man was not very helpful as he knew nothing of motors and could not even remember whether it was a shut or open car.

It was not until the fourth day of the enquiry that the first piece of real information was brought to the station. A woman who kept a combined tobacco and newspaper shop in a small street in a different part of the town stated that a month before the murder a man answering to the Petworth description had bought a Reading street-directory from her shop. She particularly remembered the dark, sunken eyes, the high cheekbones and hollow cheeks. It was after six o'clock when he had entered the shop and she had felt a thrill of alarm at the sinister appearance of her evening customer. He was wearing a long black great-coat and a black felt hat pulled down over his eyes. She was extremely glad when he had gone. Questioned about his voice, the woman answered that she noticed nothing peculiar about it, neither a special harshness nor a foreign accent. Just as she was leaving the station, she turned and added thoughtfully, "And what's more I think I've seen him before. Years ago."

Dewar tried to conceal the eagerness in his voice as he said, "Can you remember when and where?"

The woman sat down again and began to talk to herself, aloud. "It wasn't last year nor the year before. It might have been the year before that. No. I don't believe that it was, but why I don't believe that it was I'm sure I don't know. It was '27 or '26 or '25. I know. Why didn't I think of it before? It was just before Derby Day and my old man had drawn Sansovino in the sweep at the Wheel and Spokes, and I saw that man in the street just after the draw, and I said to my old man that meeting a face like that wouldn't bring us any luck, but it did and Sansovino won. What year would that be?"

"Sansovino's year," said the sergeant on duty. "That would be 1924."

"Then 1924 it was. I remember it as plain as can be, seeing that face in the street outside the old Wheel. It fair gave me the horrors."

"You're sure it was the same one?" asked Dewar.

"Well, sir, it's a good time ago and I wouldn't go into a witness-box and swear to it. But I'm sure in my own mind, all the same."

That evening, Dewar, his brain reeling, returned to Scotland Yard to consult Superintendent Bone.

"I'm absolutely beat, sir," were his first words on entering the Superintendent's office.

"Not for the first time, young Dewar," answered Bone, with a lazy laugh. He was in the highest good-humour, having that very morning organized the arrest of the biggest cocaine-dealer in the West End of London, a man who had evaded capture for nearly seven years.

"What's your trouble now? Find the air of Reading healthy?"

"I found the air of Reading perfectly confounded."

Bone smiled genially. "I thought you would. Tell me all about it."

But his smile gradually faded as Dewar's story progressed until it vanished altogether and was replaced by an unusually serious and thoughtful expression.

"Well, upon my soul," was his comment at the end. "If that doesn't beat the band. I don't wonder you're a bit out of your depth. What a business!"

There was a long silence while the Superintendent pondered and Dewar sat and did nothing. He was tired of worrying his brain over the whale affair, and was becoming more and more firmly convinced that the murders were the disconnected and irresponsible acts of a homicidal maniac.

"So we're at a dead end again," observed Dewar.

"Not quite. Cheer up," answered Bone. "The man with the horrid face is coming slowly to the surface. I wonder if it's a coincidence. The very man who makes enquiries at Petworth or if not the very man, at any rate someone very like him—turns up at Reading a short time before the poor little chemist is shot. That's odd."

"And he turned up in Reading four years before. That's odder still," said Dewar.

"Yes. I admit that is extraordinary. I can't fit that into any part of the puzzle."

"If it comes to that, can you fit Cullen into any part at all? Where does a harmless, Methodist tradesman who's never been further from Reading than Lyme Regis connect with a gang of murdering cutthroats and I.D.B.s and gunrunners from Jo'burg and Angola and Belgian Congo?"

"Most eloquently put," said Bone, "and quite unanswerable. We can't connect him. The human brain staggers at the thought of having to try. But there's the cardboard and the bullet. There's the coincidence of the man's age—an elderly man like the rest—and the reappearance of the Petworth man."

"I've got two ideas, sir," said Dewar suddenly. "The Petworth description confirmed by the Reading woman, is a perfect description of a madman. The black eyes and hollow cheeks and sinister get-up, why it might be an exact description of a Jack the Ripper."

"Of course it is. But you must remember that these homicidal maniacs always have some queer, insane motive for their murders. Jack only killed street women because he believed that he had a divine mission to kill street women. But I refuse to think that this man believes he has a divine mission to kill financiers like Skinner, emigrant-farmers like Rice and Wilton, tramps and highly respectable Methodist chemists. It would be too much of a mission altogether. No. There's always a crazy motive for their craziness. What's your other idea?"

"That a whole batch of pistols were manufactured with the same flaw in the barrel, so that the bullets fired by all of them had the identical scoring."

Bone picked up his telephone. "Sergeant on duty? Superintendent Bone speaking. Ask the gunsmith sergeant to come to my room for a moment—what's his name—Carter—that's it."

"I doubt if it's possible, Dewar, but it may be. Carter will know, anyway. Ah, Carter, come in. I've got a point for you. Would it be possible for a whole batch of pistols to be manufactured with an identical flaw in the barrel so that all their bullets were identically scored?"

Sergeant Carter answered promptly, "it wouldn't be impossible, sir, in the sense that it wouldn't be impossible for two men to have identical finger-prints. But it's so unlikely as to be impossible for all practical purposes."

"Thank you. That is all I wanted, Carter."

"That's that," said Dewar.

"Yes. It brings us back to where we were before. You're quite certain that this Cullen never went abroad?"

"That's one point that they're all unanimous about. They seem to think it's rather a comical idea. Dozens of people came forward to say that he never left Reading, except to take his family to the seaside for the summer holidays, enough to account for almost every moment of his life since he was born. It's one of the few things I've felt comparatively certain about since Skinner was killed."

Bone lay back in his chair. "He's the first man whose movements between 1900 and 1905 we've been able to trace and they can't be described as very helpful. In fact they can hardly be described as movements at all. Mr Cullen was what you might call a static sort of bird. The crux in this case lies, as we know, or think we know, somewhere in these years. Cullen is concerned in the crux. Cullen was never out of Reading. Therefore the crux is in Reading. How about that for reasoning?"

Dewar laughed. "It's flawless, sir. But I don't believe it."

"Nor do I. And that just shows that logic is a pretty useless thing when it comes to a pinch. I'm certain that the solution of all our troubles is in South Africa. Logic proves to me that it must be in Reading. I prefer my own opinion. By the way, the missing cardboard numbers—which are missing?"

"Six, seven and eight, sir. Oliver Maddock was Five and Cullen is Nine."

"The obvious thing is that three of the men are dead, whoever they were. After all 1905 is twenty-four years ago and it isn't surprising that some of the gang have died in the interval."

"I find it difficult to associate the harmless Cullen with the word 'gang.'"

"Or with great financiers like Skinner or scum like Henry Maddock."

"In fact, sir, Cullen has upset everything," said Dewar irritably. "He's out of the picture, or rather his being in the picture has put everything else out."

A constable knocked and entered. "The Assistant Commissioner wishes to see you, sir." The Superintendent made a comical grimace and heaved himself out of his chair.

"In the meantime, sir?" asked Dewar.

"Oh, in the meantime, I should go back to Reading and see if you can pick up anything more about the Petworth man and Cullen's life. Give it another week. By that time Number Ten will probably come along. I expect Number Ten will be an Archbishop or a Mother Superior. So long, young Dewar," and the Superintendent rolled out of the door like an Atlantic liner in a heavy sea.

In a gloomy and pessimistic frame of mind Dewar returned to Reading. The series of undetected murders was becoming an obsession to him. It was by far the longest period that he had ever been on a single case without making the slightest progress and the natural depression caused by failure was accentuated by the incessant brooding over the same set of circumstances and the same set of characters. To make matters worse, out of the fog and obscurity which had enshrouded the case from the beginning, there was gradually evolving in Dewar's mind the dark and shadowy figure of the Murderer. The more he thought about him, the blacker and more brilliant his eyes seemed to grow. His sunken cheeks grew even more hollow. His cheek-bones were higher and more prominent. Dewar had only to shut his eyes to see the tall figure in the long black overcoat with the black hat pulled down over his forehead, moving with quiet and relentless steps from town to town, from country to country, from continent to continent in unwavering pursuit of the men who had wronged him five and twenty years ago. The long thin knife would be in his breast pocket, the air pistol with the flaw in the barrel in his side pocket. The quietness and the simplicity of it were so terrifying. No one had seen a figure approaching the victims. No one had seen a figure hastening from the scenes of the murders. In every case the moment had been carefully chosen, the method of retreat skilfully prepared, and when the moment had arrived, each murder committed with ruthless efficiency and each retreat effected without fuss or hurry.

"Like a cat in the night hunting a bird," thought Dewar. "There will be some anxious moments if we ever get up with him. Peter the Painter was a clumsy amateur compared with this fellow."

And then suddenly an idea struck him. He had gradually built up this picture of the Murderer from the circumstances of each successive murder, the secrecy, the success, the get-away, the instantaneous death of each victim, the total absence of bungle, in fact the complete and perfect efficiency of each crime. And he was asking himself to believe that the man who possessed the qualities necessary for these murders actually made the grotesque and unbelievable mistake of shooting the wrong Maddock.

Inspector Dewar was sitting in an Inner Circle Underground train on his way to Paddington when this thought occurred to him. He was astonished at its simplicity and so flabbergasted at his stupidity in not thinking of it before that before he had recovered himself the train had carried him past Paddington to the Edgware Road station.

He looked at the name of the station with a smile.

"That's an omen," he said to himself, although like a hard-headed Scot he did not in the least believe in such superstitions. "That's an omen against my going to Reading today."

He left the Underground at Edgware Road, took a bus to King's Cross and in an hour was walking briskly in the direction of Greenlawns. In answer to his ring a young man whom he instantly guessed to be Bill Maddock came to the front door.

"Are you Mr Maddock?" he asked and the young man answered defiantly, "Yes, and if you're from a newspaper I'll kick you down the steps."

"I'm not a reporter," answered Dewar. "I'm from Scotland Yard and I want to ask you a question."

The young man's defiance had given place to a scowl. "If it's about my father you can save your breath. I wasn't here when it happened and I don't know anything about it and I wouldn't tell you anything even if I did."

"It's not about your father," answered Dewar soothingly. "It's about your uncle Oliver."

"Oh, that old story!" exclaimed Bill Maddock petulantly. "I thought that was over and done with. Good God! what a time our family's had lately. Well, come in, Mr Sexton Blake, and fire away."

"I won't keep you more than a moment," said Dewar. "I want to know if you ever heard from your father or anyone else any details of the early life of your uncle Oliver. Where he lived, what he did and so on."

"He lived in St Andrews."

"Yes, I know. But before that."

"Before that? Oh, Lord, I don't know. He's always lived in St Andrews ever since I knew him. Let's see. We came home in 1906—I was a baby then—two years old. Uncle Oliver went to Scotland before that, I'm sure. As for what he did before that, he was a schoolmaster in London or somewhere, I believe, and he did tutoring and odd jobs. But I don't really know. Somehow we never took very much interest in him. He was a stodgy old cove."

"Would your sister know any more?"

"Less I should think. She's a year younger than me and never knows anything."

"Is there anyone who might be able to tell me?"

The young man pondered. "Well, he had some sort of a housekeeper in Scotland. She might know. And then there's Aunt Emilia, but we're not on speaking terms with her."

"Is she your father's sister?"

"No, my mother's. She's a Mrs George Angus and she lives somewhere in London—Ilford I think. She hates my father but she might be able to tell you something about Oliver."

And with this scanty information Dewar had to be content. There was nothing more to be got from Bill Maddock.

The telephone directory revealed a George Angus, cabinetmaker, 424 Bridge Road, Ilford, and the Inspector proceeded to Ilford, having first taken the precaution of ringing up Scotland Yard and leaving a message for the Superintendent of his change of plan.

Mrs George Angus was a comely, middle-aged woman who had obviously been a beauty in her day. She proved ready enough to talk about Oliver Maddock, but the Inspector saw a tightening of the lip and a flash in the eye whenever the conversation turned in the direction of his brother.

"Yes, sir," said Mrs Angus. "I remember Oliver Maddock in the old days, although I don't suppose I saw him more than half a dozen times altogether. My poor sister Mary, you see, had a weak chest and we, the rest of us, saved and scraped enough to send her to Africa on a voyage. Would to God we never had. We never had another happy moment over her. She went to Africa and—and got married. She never came back. That man killed her, I know, by his cruelty and his ways. But before that, Mr Oliver used to come round with news of her and her—his brother. Until 1900, when he stopped coming. I didn't know why at the time. But I found out afterwards. There was no news from—him. He was in prison."

Dewar nodded. "I know. And what was Oliver Maddock doing at that time?"

"He was a schoolmaster in a school at Tottenham. But he left London soon afterwards and I never saw him again."

"When do you think he would have left?"

"It was after 1900, sir, because in that year he came once or twice with news of his brother. I think it would have been 1901."

"And you don't know where he went to?"

"I'm afraid not, sir. He told me at the time but I didn't pay much attention. I think it was out of London. He had got a new post and a better one. But it's a long time ago to remember anything exactly."

"Of course it is, madam. I am very grateful for what you've told me."

Dewar left Bridge Road, Ilford, no wiser than he had reached it, sent a telegram to the St Andrews police and resumed his interrupted journey to Reading.

On the following day, just as he was leaving his hotel to make a round of the garages on the chance that the Petworth man had bought petrol in the town, he was handed a telegram. It was from St Andrews and Dewar read:

"Maddocks housekeeper Mrs Auchterlonie states that Maddock was formerly schoolteacher at St Botolphs school Reading Berkshire signed Anderson inspector."

CHAPTER XX

The Kettle of Fish is a Red Herring

Dewar was almost dizzy as he walked slowly back into the hotel lounge and sat down on a sofa. After all these months the incredible had happened. Two facts had made a connection. Of all the hundreds of facts that he had discovered no single pair had had the remotest connection with each other until this moment. He had almost given up, believing that he would ever find the faintest vestige of relationship between any of them, and, suddenly, out of the blue had come the telegram from St Andrews and—click! two facts had met and slipped into place. The murdered Maddock had been a Reading schoolmaster; the murdered Cullen had been a Reading chemist. Now things would move. He put a trunk call through to Scotland Yard and reported the news to Bone and had the gratification of impressing even that worldly-wise and experienced gentleman. "Say that again," he said after an appreciable pause, and when Dewar had said it again, he said "I'll come down," and rang off.

One or two zealous policemen on the Great West Road had to step hastily out of the way of the big Vauxhall police car in which the Superintendent travelled to Reading, in order to avoid an early and untimely end, and at the police station in Reading, Dewar was astounded at the nimbleness with which the stout Superintendent sprang out and dived into Inspector Avory's office. The physical lethargy for which he was famous at Scotland Yard had gone. The great detective who had never been seen to run since he became a sergeant almost pattered into the C.I.D. room, threw himself on to an ordinary hard chair which creaked ominously, looked at Dewar and then broke into a long and hearty laugh.

"Well, young Dewar, we're a pair of mugs. Too clever by half, aren't we? What a business! I doubt if I shall ever hear the end of this. So it was Oliver Maddock after all. And we never took the slightest trouble about the poor man. Well, well."

He mopped his brow.

"What do you make of it, sir?" asked Dewar.

"Make of it? It's as plain as a pikestaff. It's been as plain as a pikestaff from the beginning if we hadn't been so extremely clever. Why, the man who shot Oliver M. meant to shoot Oliver M., that's all. We jumped on to Henry, like a ton of bricks just because Henry was a wrong 'un and so we got landed with quite a different kettle of fish. All that South Africa stuff is another show altogether."

"It seems incredible, sir. Digging up Jan Hendrick and all."

"That was the worst bit of bad luck we had. It kept us on the wrong track just when we might have begun to cast round for another line. No, my lad. I never was so wrong in my life. The key to all these murders isn't in Africa. It's in Reading."

"You'll probably think I'm being disrespectful, sir——"

"I certainly will. But never mind. Go ahead."

"Well, sir, don't you think you're jumping rather far ahead?"

"I may be, you canny Scotsman, but I tell you this. I'm so fed up with failure on this case that I'm prepared to jump a mile—or try to"—he glanced down at his spreading figure—"on the chance of getting out of this tangle. I'm going to follow it up. Inspector Avory, lead the way to St Botolph's School. Dewar and I are with you." The registers of the secondary school of St Botolph's were dug out of a dusty and dingy office by a bewildered official of the local education authority and displayed to the detectives. The examination lasted about one and a half minutes. From January, 1901 until December, 1905 one of the assistant masters at the school had been called Oliver George Maddock. He had lived at 214 Westhill Parade.

At this address they found nothing. The house had changed hands often since 1905 and there was no one in the neighbouring houses or among the small tradesmen in the vicinity who remembered Maddock. "Never mind," said Bone cheerfully. "We wouldn't have learnt much anyway from them. The next thing is to find some of the other names—Skinner, Rice and Wilton."

"What an extraordinary crew to be mixed up together," said Dewar. "It isn't often that you find a gang of crooks including two men like Maddock and Cullen."

"Not as they were a year ago. But we don't know what they were like twenty-odd years ago. You've known almost as many people as I have, young Dewar, who are more virtuous today than they used to be. Whatever it was that these two were doing between 1900 and 1905, it was something that brought them to a violent end at last. So it couldn't have been all beer and skittles." He wrinkled his brows. "I can see lots of jobs in which a chemist would have been very useful. But it's harder to see the part played by a secondary schoolmaster, unless of course his being a schoolmaster was all a blind and Oliver provided the brains of the gang. He was a brainy bird, wasn't he, Dewar?"

"He was a great reader of books, sir."

"Well, so are you, so that doesn't count for much. Lead on once again, Mr Avory. The town hall is our place now for an hour or two." The Superintendent's next objective was the Register of Parliamentary Voters for the first five years of the century, but here he met with a check. The Register had been compiled in 1898 and therefore did not include voters who had settled in the district after that date. Albert Cullen's father and grandfather were included but none of the other names. The Register of voters for Municipal elections was equally unproductive. Bone refused to be depressed.

"Street directories, please," was his next request and a few moments later he gave a loud crow of delight and slapped Avory heavily on the shoulder.

"What about this, my lad? Skinner, Aloysius, 34 Well Avenue."

"What date is that?" cried Dewar eagerly and Bone grinned.

"That excites even Dumbartonshire, does it? It's 1902. Give us the next one. Yes, here he is. 1903. And the next. Yes. And the next. No. There's no Skinner here. So he lived here in 1902, 1903 and 1904." He broke off and looked at Dewar. "By George, what a lot of trouble we'd have saved if we hadn't been quite so smart."

Dewar was inclined to protest. "Even if we'd traced Oliver and Skinner back to Reading we mightn't have got any further without this Cullen murder."

"Nonsense," exclaimed Bone. "We've got the whole case in our hands now, even without Cullen. Now that we know all these men lived simultaneously in Reading at the exact period we suspected——" He broke off and stared at Dewar and then whistled. "I say. That is rather extraordinary. Do you realise that we arrived at the fatal period of 1900 to 1905 by the argument that it was the only period at which Skinner could have met Henry Maddock, and now Henry has dropped clean out of it but the period still remains. That's very queer. However," he went on more briskly, "it doesn't really matter if we arrive at the truth through a mistake in the argument, so long as we don't let the folk upstairs hear about it. They're cross enough as it is about the Skinner business."

Inspector Avory smiled. "I'm delighted, sir, to hear that one of you London gentlemen can make mistakes."

Bone wagged a heavy forefinger at the Reading inspector. "And let it be a lesson to you, young man, that we're so clever that even our mistakes lead us to the truth. But don't tell the Commissioner. What was I saying? Oh, yes. Now that we know that these men lived simultaneously in Reading it shouldn't take us very long to find out what they were all doing and what were the names of the others. And yet," he shook his head slowly, "there's still something funny about it. There's something that sticks in my throat."

"What is it, sir?" asked Dewar. Bone looked up at him. "Young man, I know what your trouble is. You've given up thinking about this case. Your idea is that I'm here to do the thinking. So I am. But it's no reason why you shouldn't try as well."

Dewar was taken aback by this reproof and muttered, "I do think, but you think so much faster than I do." He could not have chosen a more happy defence. The Superintendent was delighted. He lay back and purred with satisfaction.

"What was it you find funny about the case?" put in Avory, and Bone sat up again alertly.

"Why, this," he answered. "We are assuming that these men were assembled in Reading for some illegal purpose. Personally I am inclined to make a guess that they were coiners. Do you remember the great half-crown faking about that period? Before your time perhaps. Anyway, let us simply say for an illegal purpose. Some time in 1904 or 1905 the gang breaks up or is broken up. Skinner clears in 1904 but Maddock stays on until 1905 and Cullen never clears at all. And none of them change their names."

"Perhaps the gang wasn't broken up," suggested Dewar. "Perhaps it just dissolved itself."

"But our theory presupposes treachery and one man serving a long sentence. By the bye, Dewar, that's another thing we've neglected. Curse and confound Henry Maddock and his South African experiences. I was never so led off on a wild-goose chase in my life."

"It led to a murderer," said Dewar.

"I know it did. But that was a fluke, coupled with your reasoning powers," he added hastily. "But we've neglected that list of long term men who were sent down before 1905 and not released till after 1925. Have you got it with you?"

"Yes, sir."

"We must look into that. But so far as I can recall it, most of them were sweetheart crimes of one sort or another."

"Four of them, sir. And there was a street fight and two burglars."

"Not much trace of an organised crowd in that lot. You came across nothing of the sort in their trials?"

"No, sir."

Bone considered for a moment. "The most promising lines seem to me to find out Skinner's occupation at the time and the whereabouts of Rice and Wilton. If you take Skinner, Dewar, I'll rout about after the other two. And perhaps Avory would look up his Assize records for these years and make a list of his major convictions. It might help. Meet again in Avory's office at seven o'clock this evening."

Dewar's share of the afternoon's work did not last him long. The clerk of the Reading Chamber of Commerce was an ardent student of detective fiction and was thrilled at the prospect of collaborating, however humbly, with a real detective from Scotland Yard. With trembling fingers and a blush of excitement which stretched all the way round to the back of his neck, he delved eagerly among the files of the Chamber and in less than ten minutes produced the required information. Aloysius Skinner had been managing director of the Van Doone Dyeworks, Haarlem House, Reading, from 1902 to 1904. He had left to become a director of a firm in London. The Van Doone Dyeworks had prospered, had been turned into a public company, had languished under German competition, had produced explosives during the war, had languished again and finally been absorbed into the Imperial Cochineal Company. So far as the clerk knew, Skinner had taken no active part in industry in Reading since his departure from the town in 1904.

"Have you any personal information about him?" asked Dewar and the clerk hesitated.

Dewar glanced round and lowered his voice impressively. "It's a murder case, you know."

"What!" exclaimed the young man in a corresponding whisper. "It's not *the* Skinner of Imperial Cochineal! The man who was——"

"The very same," said Dewar assuming as melodramatic an attitude as he could manage. The clerk capitulated with alacrity.

"I'll fetch the confidential record," he hissed and went on tip-toe to the safe. Dewar suppressed a grin.

"There you are," said the youth. "Skinner, Aloysius. Antecedents unknown. Able. Apparently honest. Resigned in 1904 on promotion to London."

Dewar turned to the company of which Skinner had been managing director and read "Van Doone Dyeworks. Haarlem House. Founded 1901. Strong financial backing. Pays high wages. Reputable Continental connections." And then in another hand was written, "1904. A1 position," and then followed a record of the vicissitudes of the company down to its absorption by Imperial Cochineal.

"They thought well of him in Reading business circles anyway," thought Dewar. "At least, they had nothing against him."

On the off chance he walked round to Well Avenue and made inquiries among the neighbours. But as he expected no one remembered the name. At the Dyeworks he had no better luck. The staff had been reduced during the lean years of German competition, had been quadrupled and quintupled during the war, reduced again in the post-war slump and finally altered by the amalgamation. The result was that the employee with the longest period of service had joined the firm as recently as 1910.

With this result of his afternoon's work, Dewar returned to the police station where Avory was waiting. Bone marched in a few minutes later. "Got 'em," he announced. "Rice and Wilton. Speculated in farm produce in 1906 and went bankrupt. No wonder we couldn't track them, looking for sheep farmers or shepherds. They were country born lads who came to town and tried to make a fortune."

"That explains what the innkeeper at Petworth said," exclaimed Dewar. "About their sitting in corners and working out figures on bits of paper."

"Things are beginning to fit together, my lad, aren't they?" said Bone. "What have you done?"

The Superintendent listened and then made a grimace. "You haven't been half so successful as I have. I've found a couple of bankrupts while you've only found an honest man. We've no use for honest men in this show. Honest men don't go and get killed like this. What about you, Avory, my lad?"

The Reading inspector had a large sheet of paper in front of him, covered with pencil notes. "There were eighteen sentences of seven years or more at the Reading Assizes between 1900 and 1905," he said.

"Eighteen," remarked Bone. "What a deucedly wicked city this must be."

"It was before I became an inspector," said Avory, primly.

"Go ahead. Start with the biggest sentences."

"Then there were three men hanged. Hobson, Smith and Horrock."

"Leave them out. We're looking for a long term man, but execution is too long a term for our purpose."

"There were four lifers. Thomas, Bartlett, Vernon and Box."

Dewar started up. "What did you say? Box?"

"Yes."

Bone and Avory looked at him in astonishment.

"What's the matter, young Dewar?"

"Box is one of the names in my list."

"What list?"

"Of men who were sentenced before 1905 and didn't come out till after 1925."

CHAPTER XXI

Harry Box

"Well, well," murmured Superintendent Bone. "The facts do seem to be fitting in at last. So Box was a Reading man and Box is one of our seven heroes who served more than twenty years. Finish your list, Mr Inspector, if you please. We'd better hear them all before we make up our minds."

Avory read slowly his list of major sentences, ticking off each one as the London superintendent shook his head. In no instance was there a trace of an organization of law-breakers and in only one case was more than one man convicted of being concerned in the same crime and that was a safe-breaking by two well-known Metropolitan burglars.

At the end of the recital Bone said, "Now for Mr Box. By the way, Dewar, you looked up his trial, didn't you?"

"Yes, sir. But it was before the Cullen murder and we weren't much interested in Reading then. If it had been afterwards——"

Bone said nothing but Dewar felt that he was being silently censured. He admitted to himself that when he had searched the records for news of the trials, he had not particularly noted the places where the crimes had been committed. The South African obsession had got hold of him as well as Bone.

"Box killed a man for going off with his wife. He was an engineer by profession and apparently a rather superior sort of chap." Avory was speaking. "I gather that there was a good deal of sympathy for him as the man he killed was a thoroughly bad lot. Attractive in a flashy sort of way and got on well with women, but otherwise a complete rotter."

"Has Box any relatives in Reading now?" asked Bone.

"That I don't know. He worked in the engine-yards, a foreman-fitter, and was doing well."

"And the woman?"

"There again I don't know. But I fancy she must have left the district soon afterwards."

The Superintendent sighed. "It's most unsatisfactory. What has the murder of a man like that got to do with our little lot? They can't all have run away with the man's wife, at least I suppose they could have, but it's extremely improbable. You can't produce a party of coiners, can you, Avory, or a couple of race-gangs? That would be far better than this Frenchified crime of passion—isn't that what they call it, Dewar?—which doesn't help at all."

"It hardly sounds as if it can be the man," said Dewar.

"It certainly doesn't. But it is a remarkable coincidence. We deduce a twenty-year convict and one of the only seven twenty-yearers who corresponds to the dates comes from this very town. Confound it," he cried suddenly, "we only deduced that twenty-year business from Henry Maddock's movements. Dewar, I'm getting muddled. Avory, this is an unforgettable day in your official career. You've seen a London superintendent muddled."

"I've seen that before, sir, but I've never heard one admit it before."

Dewar interposed, "As a matter of fact, sir, the dates are all right. Cullen is our sheet-anchor. Cullen never left Reading, therefore the others must have come to Reading. Skinner was only here from 1902 to 1904, therefore those must have been the years. And the convict must have been an extra-long-term man after all."

Bone's face lightened. "Of course. My mind is now perfectly clear. Avory, your last glimpse of a muddled Superintendent has gone for ever. We will exclude the attractive theory that Cullen's visits to Lyme Regis in the summer holidays were for the purpose of organizing an international ring of eau-de-cologne smugglers and concentrate for a moment on Box. Have you anything more there about him, Avory?"

"Not here, sir. But it's all in the records." In a few moments a sergeant came in with a complete account of the trial of Box, a duplicate of which Dewar had studied at Scotland Yard. Bone glanced rapidly over it, muttering comments aloud as he went. "Hm! Good-looking fellow ... superior type ... not guilty ... denied all knowledge ... man shot in head and chest ... Box swore he was out testing a motor-car ... no one saw him ... dead man had lots of enemies ... pistol found in Box's rooms under floor ... damned silly place to hide it ... found guilty ... sentence ... outburst in dock and so on. That's all. Box's record. Son of Lancashire engineer, brother in Mercantile Marine ... married Elsie, daughter of John Carpenter, baker, in Newbury. Fine footballer, hot-tempered and reserved. Bound over in January, 1901, for striking a man who said that Lancashire was a county of cowards. Wesleyan Methodist. Regular chapel-goer. Twice received bonus from engine-company for inventions."

Bone looked up. "That's a bird's-eye biography of a rather remarkable young man. It's the biography of a murderer but it doesn't sound to me like the biography of a crook. But you never can tell. Certainly an engineer and a chemist would be a useful pair in any party. Skinner would manage the finance, Rice and Wilton, lord knows what part they would play, and as for Oliver Maddock——" Bone sighed comically. "What a crew! Well, we'd better send out a call to pull in Box. It won't do any harm. We can always get up the Petworth man to have a look at him. Will you see to it, Avory. I shall go across to Newbury and see if I can have a talk with John Carpenter, or better still with Elsie Box."

"And what shall I do, sir?" asked Dewar.

"Go to a movie."

"I'd sooner come with you."

"I can't resist the compliment," said Bone. "You shall come with me."

At Newbury they found it easy to trace John Carpenter. He had become in the passage of long years a local celebrity. Over seventy years of age, he had been a member of the Urban District Council for more than forty-five years, and his white hair and beard and his kindly old blue eyes were known to every man, woman and child in the parish. The first boy that Dewar asked directed the police-car promptly and unerringly to the small detached villa where the old man lived. John Carpenter was sitting in the evening sun at his front door and he eyed the car with a benign curiosity. The Superintendent looked for an appreciable number of seconds at the placid, handsome old veteran, and then he swore under his breath. "Damn it, Dewar. Sometimes I loathe our job." Then he jumped out, pushed open the iron gate and walked up the narrow gravel path.

"My name is Bone, and I have come here upon the most distasteful errand I have ever had to perform," he began at once.

"If you are doing your duty, the errand should not be distasteful," was the quiet answer.

"Well said," answered Bone, and paused, seeking for words.

"Your errand, sir?"

"It is to awaken old and sad memories."

"Mine?" The old voice had sunk a little. Bone nodded. John Carpenter clenched his fists a little and then relaxed them slowly. "Go on," he said, with a deep sigh. "What is it you want?"

Again Bone found it difficult to know how to begin and the old man helped him out. "It's about my daughter, I suppose, and her man?"

"Yes."

"She's dead, you know."

"No. I didn't. I came to ask—I wanted to know——" Dewar had never seen his chief so moved.

"She came home to me to die. It was in 1922. She had consumption. I buried her over there." He pointed vaguely towards the south.

"And her husband ..."

"He came here in 1925. I saw him. I spoke to him. I haven't seen him since."

"You don't know where he is now or what he's doing?"

"No."

"Did he seem to you to be quite normal when you saw him?"

"Normal? You mean sane?"

"Yes."

"No. I don't know who you are, sir, but you've asked me a question and I'll answer it. In my opinion Harry Box was mad."

"But in the old days?"

"Ah, the old days. There wasn't a finer lad in the southern counties. Hot-tempered, but straight as a die. But that was years ago. Before that man came to Reading, the man who caused all the trouble."

"The man who was shot?"

"Yes. But it's an old story and my Elsie's dead and Harry's mad. It happened long ago." The old man stood up. "You have indeed awakened old and sad memories, sir. Is your errand finished?"

"Yes," answered Bone slowly.

The two hardened, experienced Scotland Yard men drove back to Reading in silence.

CHAPTER XXII

Sir Harold Crawhall, Number Ten

The hue and cry for Harry Box ran up and down the country without any result. Bone and Dewar had returned to London, confident that the discovery of Box was the final step in the long investigation. But Box refused to be discovered. He had been so long out of the world that he had no familiar haunts, no old friends, no well-known habits which would give the police something to go on. His appearance, as portrayed by prison photographs and records, was one that lent itself singularly well to disguise. The blackness of his eyebrows was a prominent feature. Once bleached or dyed, his face would lose half its distinctness. A little wax would alter the hollowness of his cheeks beyond recognition, and then there would be nothing to look out for except the sunken brightness of his eyes. If he was careful not to look people in the face, even that could be minimized.

Lancashire was combed from end to end on the chance that he had returned to some unknown relatives and a special force of plain-clothes men was drafted into Reading in case the series of murders should be continued in that town.

Bone's final words to Dewar had been advice to take his mind off the case altogether. He put his subordinate on to an intricate case of ware-house robberies with the words, "Cut out the Box affair altogether, young Dewar. We've spent three months trying to fit all these people together in order to get the murderer. Now I think we've got the murderer and he'll help us to fit all the people together. It's the other way round. Run along to Millbank and have a look at Levison's warehouse. They've lifted five thousand pounds' worth of furs."

"Any tips, sir?"

"There was a big fur steal about this time last year and the stuff from it ought to be reaching the Leipzig Fair this year. Those fellows work a year in advance. That's all I can tell you. Run along. Box will settle all our troubles."

But Henry Box obstinately declined to be found. A fortnight elapsed and the Superintendent began to get worried. At any moment Number Ten in the deadly series might appear, and there was no reason to suppose that Number Ten would provide him with any better results than One, Two, Three, Four, Five and Nine. Of course there was no certainty that there would be a Number Ten. On the other hand there was equally no certainty that the series would stop at Ten or Twenty.... Bone almost shuddered and once again cursed himself for his folly in being misled by the red herring of Henry Maddock. On the fourteenth day after Bone's return from Reading the news of Number Ten reached Scotland Yard.

Sir Harold Crawhall, of Warrington Lodge, near Bradford, had been shot in peculiar circumstances. Sir Harold was an extremely rich, self-made man who had entered the woollen trade comparatively late in life and had quickly increased an already large fortune. After the War, in the course of which he had prospered exceedingly, he had bought Warrington Lodge from an impoverished earl and settled down as a country gentleman. His wealth made a considerable mark, even in a part of England where wealthy industrialists are common, and his entertainments at Warrington Lodge in the short space of nine years became proverbial in the district. Sir Harold insisted on champagne being served with every meal at which a guest was present, not counting early morning tea as a meal, and his afternoon parties in the summer often led to curious scenes of hilarity and eccentricity.

On the afternoon in question, Sir Harold was receiving a large throng of friends and acquaintances, the large majority of whom had driven out from Bradford rather than from the neighbouring country-houses. For Warrington Lodge had found that even Pommery 1914 cannot buy everything. It was Sir Harold's custom on these occasions to stand, in morning coat, striped trousers and white spats, lavender tie and gardenia buttonhole, at the top of a short flight of broad, marble steps in the garden and there to shake hands with anyone who wanted to shake the knightly hand. And a lot of people availed themselves of the privilege before edging away self-consciously in the direction of the tables which were set out under the ancient oak trees. It was usual for the marble steps to be less thronged and the lawn under the oaks to be proportionately more thronged as the afternoon advanced. At about half-past five, just as Sir Harold was thinking of making a move himself in the direction of the tables, a latecomer walked briskly up the marble steps and engaged the host in conversation. Only one person in all that party could be found who had happened to be looking in the direction of the steps during those fatal moments. The rest had forgotten their host completely.

The solitary observer, a Mrs Crampton, the wife of a wool-merchant, stated that she had no idea why she happened to be looking at Sir Harold. She just happened to be. The man shook hands with Sir Harold and then they talked for about half a minute, as near as Mrs Crampton could judge. Then Sir Harold put his hand on his heart with a queer, jerky movement and sank very slowly forward first on to his knees and then gradually sprawling face downwards on the steps. The stranger stood in front of him until Sir Harold lay still and then he turned and shouted in the direction of the crowd on the lawn, "Sir Harold is ill, I'll go for a doctor," and with that he sprang over a flower-bed and raced round the house in the direction of the front avenue.

The guests, after a moment of petrified astonishment, tumbled in a confused mass over the lawn in the direction of the steps, with the exception of one or two elderly gentlemen, who realized that there was nothing they could do and that it would be wiser and more helpful if they kept their heads and did nothing. They accordingly kept their heads and refilled their glasses. The remainder reached the foot of the steps in a body and halted in a body, each individual being uncertain of the procedure with invalids. One or two exclaimed, "Stand back. Give him air," a not very helpful contribution, as everyone was determined in any case to stand back. Then, after an awkward moment or two, a middle-aged man who had served in the War stepped forward and went up towards the body. He lifted the head and shoulders on to the same level as the rest and began to loosen the collar. Then he stopped and said, "My God! he's dead." Even then he did not notice the tear in the immaculate morning-coat where the bullet had entered and it was not until nearly half an hour later when a doctor had arrived and the body had been carried into the house that the truth was discovered. And it was not until then that the square of white cardboard on which the word Ten was written and which was found lying beside the body was associated with the murder.

The absence of sound was attributed to an air-pistol fired in an atmosphere charged with the incessant popping of the corks of Pommery 1914. It was reckoned that a hundred and seventy motor-cars were parked round about the front gate of Warrington Lodge, and the car in which the murderer escaped was not identified. Owner-drivers are so common that no one pays any attention to a man driving his own car, provided that he is dressed well and that his car is neither a ten-cylinder sports model to seat two nor a two-cylinder family model to seat ten. A motorist has to be extremely conspicuous to be noticed. The murderer had clearly taken pains not to be conspicuous and had reaped his reward.

The bullet, of course, bore the inevitable scoring which identified the crime as being one of the series. The cardboard was identified with the other cardboards. The murdered man was several years over sixty and there was no apparent motive for the crime.

Superintendent Bone read the report of the Bradford police with a heavy frown upon his usually unwrinkled forehead. He would not have confessed as much to Dewar or to anyone else, but these murders were beginning to rattle him—him, Superintendent Bone, thirty-five years in the Metropolitan Police Force. He pulled an ABC time-table from a shelf, turned up Bradford and then slowly shut it and replaced it on the shelf with a shake of his head.

He pressed a bell and asked the constable who answered it whether Inspector Dewar was in the building. In a few minutes Dewar came in. "Seen the news from Bradford?" he asked and flipped the report across to him.

"Not Number Ten?"

"Number Ten. Dewar, send a telegram to Hitchcock in Bradford and ask him if Crawhall ever lived in Reading and had any connection with Box. What was Crawhall? Do you know the name?"

"No, sir."

"From this report he seems to have been a profiteer and a very rich man. It might be that he and Skinner got away with all the money and that Box—no damn it. I won't theorize any more. I'm beginning to go back to our old theory that Box is mad and is going about killing people who he thinks looked too favourably upon his wife. Confound it, there I am theorizing again. Send off that wire, Dewar, and let me know the answer."

The answer came in less than an hour. "Crawhall was born in Reading and lived there till forty-one stop was engaged in small weaving business stop am enquiring about your second question."

The second telegram arrived two hours later.

"Crawhall's son often heard father speak of Box stop Harold Crawhall was member of jury in Box case."

CHAPTER XXIII

The Penny Drops

The two detectives read the telegram twice aloud like men in a daze. Then there were two simultaneous whistles and two hands simultaneously grabbed the telephone.

"You do it, Dewar," almost croaked the Superintendent. "I don't think I could trust myself to speak. The jury," he added in a mutter. "The jury. Good God, is it possible?" He buried his face in his hands and groaned. Dewar put through the call to Reading and sat down to wait. Bone was in a state of nervous restlessness. "I suppose I should have guessed it," he kept on saying, adding at intervals, "But I didn't, and I don't believe I ever would have."

In a few minutes the telephone operator announced that Inspector Avory was on the line. The Superintendent seized the instrument.

"Avory, is that you, Avory. Can you hear me? This is Bone, from Scotland Yard. Yes. Look here, Avory, I want you to drop everything you're doing and find out the names of the jurymen in the Box case, jurymen, members of the jury, J for jackass—yes, jury, that's it. Do you suppose there's a list somewhere? Try everybody you can think of and telephone to me as soon as you've got it. I'll wait here for it. And I say, Avory, do it as quickly as you can. There are two lives depending on it."

"Two lives?" said Dewar, after the Superintendent had put down the telephone.

"Eleven and Twelve. juries are usually composed of twelve. You're not very bright this morning, young man."

"I'm afraid I haven't been very bright over this business at all, sir."

"Neither of us have. All the same, it's unique in my experience. I never heard of a case of a man taking revenge on the jury."

"It may not be Box at all, sir."

"We shall soon know. If none of our deceased friends are on the jury then our whole theory falls to the ground. But they must be, Dewar. They must be. If they're not——" He looked helplessly round the room. "—if they're not, then I'm beat. I shall do what I've never done in my life. I shall ask the folk upstairs to transfer the whole case to one of the other Superintendents. It will need a new eye. Come back in an hour's time."

But when Dewar went back to the Superintendent's office there was no news from Reading. At six o'clock that evening Avory telephoned to say that the search of the Assize Records was still being actively prosecuted, but that there was such a mass of unsorted and unindexed documents that progress was slow.

Bone was impatient. "We can still save two lives if we hurry. We might have saved Cullen and Crawhall as well if we'd been clever, but at least we can prevent any more. If only Avory would hurry. Who knows where that devil is now with his air-pistol."

At ten o'clock there was still no news and Bone sent Dewar away to get something to eat. The fastest police-car at Scotland Yard waited hour after hour on the Embankment while Inspector Avory and a band of policemen and clerks, hungry, dusty and tired, worked feverishly in the ill-lit vaults of the Reading Town Hall in search of the document that might save two innocent lives. Somewhere in England the dark and ruthless figure of the assassin was preparing for another of his swift and deadly attacks.

When Dewar returned he tried to persuade his chief to go and have some supper. But Bone shook his head. He was looking untidy and harassed. Dewar watched him read through a document five times and not seem to understand it at the end. He jumped when the telephonebell rang and muttered an oath at the sergeant on duty who had telephoned to know if they would like some tea sent up.

At half-past one in the morning the telephone rang again. Dewar answered it. "Reading wants you, sir," said the operator.

"It's Reading, sir," said Dewar.

"You answer it."

In another moment Avory came on the line. "That you, Dewar? I've got it at last. Been the devil's own job. I'll read out the names. Ready to write them down?"

"He's got them, sir," said Dewar reaching out for a pencil. "Fire ahead, Avory. I'm ready."

"The foreman was Aloysius Skinner."

"Foreman," Dewar repeated, writing, "Foreman, Aloysius Skinner." He could see the instantaneous look of relief which shot over the Superintendent's face, smoothing out the wrinkles magically and restoring its habitual blandness and geniality.

"Members," continued Avory, "Edgar Rice, Harold Wilson Crawhall, Albert Cullen, Samuel Arthur Bentley, William Young Boyd, John Field, George John Wilton, Henry Bedford, George Alexander Smith, Oliver Michael Maddock and Spencer Wells. Got that?"

"I've got it," said Dewar, writing hard. "Hold on. The Superintendent wants to speak to you."

Bone took the receiver and spoke urgently. "You've done splendidly, Avory, but we're not half through yet. Listen. Give me the list, Dewar. Listen, Avory. There are six names on that list of yours that are new to me. Samuel Arthur Bentley; no, half a minute. That must be the tramp. His name was Sam. That leaves five. Boyd, Field, Bedford, Smith and Wells. I've every reason to think that three of those five are already dead. And I've every reason to think that if we don't hurry the other two will be dead very soon. I'm afraid you'll get no sleep tonight. I want you to start at once finding out, if you can, which of the five are dead. Dewar and I are coming down at once. When we find out which are dead the next job will be to locate the other two. Do you get all that? Good. Then we'll be down as soon as we can."

He put down the receiver and paused for a moment with his hand still on the telephone. "The last lap, Dewar, I think. We've got that connection at last. But by Jove it's taken us some time."

It was nearly three o'clock when the physically tired but mentally elated detectives arrived once more in Reading. Avory received them. "I've done two of them," were his first words, "but they were pure good luck. My men happened to know about them. I've got a man round in the newspaper office digging away among the obituary notices, but I think we'll have to wait till the morning and get hold of the registrar. He's gone away for the night and isn't expected back till tomorrow and no one seems to know where his clerk lives. He's got a new man."

"What have you found?" asked Bone.

"Henry Bedford died about ten years ago. He was a well-known citizen and one of my sergeants has a brother who used to be his chauffeur. The other one is Spencer Wells. That was a bit of luck, too, because Wells made quite a name in the War for enlisting in the mine-sweepers when he was over fifty—dyed his hair and posed as thirty-eight. Of course we all knew his real age and it made him quite a celebrity. He hit a mine in 1917, in the winter, and the ship foundered with all hands."

"Good. That only leaves John Field, George Alexander Smith and William Young Boyd. I suppose they're not in the directory?"

"No. Which looks as if they'd left the district."

"That will be the very devil," said Bone. "You see, it will put us in a terrible position. If we're going to save their lives we've got to warn them quickly, and if we can't trace them at once we'll have to advertise. And of course if we advertise Box will lie low and our best chance of getting him will be gone. We must just wait and see. Can you give us comfortable chairs till the morning, Avory? I don't think there is anything we can do in the meantime. Put a man on to the local directories and tell him to trace the years that those men lived in the town."

He looked at his watch. "Half-past three. Three and a half hours' sleep, Dewar. Breakfast at seven and a real hard day."

The London detectives spent three and a half uncomfortable hours on office chairs and awoke stiff and sore to find breakfast and a report ready for them. The man who had searched through the directories reported that the name of John Field figured from 1898 to 1917, George Alexander Smith from 1901 to 1921, William Young Boyd from 1895 to 1919.

"Not very helpful," muttered Bone as he swallowed a fried egg at a single mouthful.

The hasty meal finished, Bone asked for the man who had been making researches in the newspaper files and was told that he had not yet returned. The next move accordingly was to the newspaper office where a very exhausted and sleep-laden constable was found wading through files of old papers.

"Any luck?" asked Bone and the constable shook his head. "There's been no one of these names died in Reading between yesterday and 1914," he declared, "but I've come across them in different connections. I've made a note of them. George Alexander Smith was a Scotchman and made a speech about a man called R. Burns On 25th January, 1919. John Field retired from business in 1917 and his employees made him a presentation. He was also on the Committee of the Soldiers and Sailors' Families Association from 1914 to 1917. William Young Boyd gave £250 to the War Memorial after the war. That's the lot, sir."

"Good. Now run along and have a sleep. You want it."

"Anything else I can do, sir?" asked the constable, wistfully eyeing the great Londoner.

"I'll let you know," said Bone with a paternal hand on the young policeman's shoulder. "You've done well here."

From the newspaper office, the Superintendent proceeded to the Registrar's, found that the office did not open until ten, and, as it was then barely eight, returned to the police station. Avory had not yet arrived and his chief assistant was in charge. Bone briefly explained the urgency of the matter and outlined the plan of campaign. "I want you to get every man you can spare on to this job. I want you to send them all over the city to the houses of prominent men, town councillors, business men, that sort of person, and ask for information about the whereabouts of these men. Somebody is bound to know. Boyd was well-to-do, Field was in an engineering works, and Smith was a Scotsman so of course he was prominent," he shot a glance at the impassive Dewar, "and it should be an easy job. Send a man on a bicycle to the Castle works——"

"Closed down in 1921, sir," put in the sub-inspector.

"Damn! Never mind. Carry on with the rest. And remember! Time is everything. Whenever a man gets a bit of news, he's to bring it or telephone it at once. Now hustle."

The full information was obtained in exactly forty minutes. George Alexander Smith had returned to Scotland and died in May, 1922 at his home in Forfarshire. John Field had been living since his retirement from business at Witton House in the village of Witton near Godalming, in Surrey. William Young Boyd had settled in a house called Greytiles, about five miles from Reading in the direction of Wokingham.

Bone called for a map and examined it. Then he turned to Dewar. "I'll take Mr William Boyd and you take Mr John Field. You'll need the car. You've furthest to go. Start now. I'll ring headquarters and have a squad waiting for you in Godalming. Ah! There's Avory. Good morning, Avory, I want a car and you and four men and six pistols, please."

CHAPTER XXIV

The Nervous Mr Field

Mr John Field was enjoying an after-breakfast pipe on the lawn of Witton House, a country house some six or seven miles south of Godalming, when Inspector Dewar was announced. Mr Field was an elderly gentleman of comfortable means and comfortable habits. He had spent more than forty years of his life in hard work and he was determined to enjoy the remainder in as much ease and leisure as he could. He found the existence of a country gentleman very much to his taste and he had thrown himself with zest into the life of the village and the countryside. He was President of the local cricket club, a churchwarden, a member of the Rural District Council, Vice-President of the football club, Patron of the Boy Scouts, and had twice been asked to contest the constituency as Conservative candidate. In short, he was an extremely popular acquisition to the neighbourhood.

On receiving a pencil note, signed J. Dewar, Inspector, asking for an immediate interview, he sat up alertly and told his butler to bring the visitor at once into the garden. A visit from a policeman meant one of two things. Either he was going to be asked for a subscription to the annual police sports, a subscription that he was always delighted to give, or else his assistance as a law-abiding citizen was going to be sought and no man regarded his civic responsibilities more seriously than Mr Field. He was disagreeably surprised, therefore, when he saw the unshaven, dishevelled and dusty figure of Inspector Dewar advancing across the lawn. Mr Field was frankly not accustomed to policemen in plain clothes. He was not certain that he had ever seen one before and the absence of polished belt and shining buttons impressed him most unfavourably. As for the man's appearance it was positively slovenly. Mr Field began to bristle and he almost started to frame the opening sentences of a letter to the Chief Constable of Surrey. The brusque opening of the stranger added to his rising indignation.

"Mr Field? I must speak to you at once, in private."

"Inspector—ah—Dewar?" asked Mr Field coldly. "And what can I do for you?"

"You must come indoors at once, sir," and then Dewar, noticing the increasing stiffness of the old gentleman, moderated his tone and added, "It's a matter of the most vital importance, sir. I do beg of you to come indoors at once."

The change of tone softened Mr Field somewhat and he rose from his deck chair and led the way across the lawn without a word. Dewar could not help glancing round at the thick shrubberies and low walls that surrounded the garden and muttering to himself, "Easy as winking. Just like Greenlawns only the walls are lower."

Mr Field led the way into his library and waved the inspector into a chair. He was moving across to a cigar cabinet which stood near the window when he stopped and exclaimed, "Whatever is the meaning of that?" Dewar followed his line of vision and saw two of his men taking post behind a clump of rhododendrons between the house and the road in such a position as to command both front door and gate.

"Those are two of my men, sir. There are two others at the back."

"I think, Inspector, you had better explain what this is all about."

"I will, sir. Does the name Box convey anything to you?"

"Box? Yes it does. I was on the jury that found a man called Box guilty of murder many years ago in Reading. I shall never forget how he shook his fist at us as he left the dock."

"Exactly. That is why I am here. Do you know that out of that jury which found Harry Box guilty only two are alive today. And you are one of them."

"Indeed?" Mr Field only took a conventional interest in the longevity of his fellow-jurors. "I am fortunate to have survived the others."

"Fortunate is exactly the word," answered Dewar grimly. "Out of the other ten, only two died peacefully in their beds and one was drowned in a mine-sweeper during the war."

"Ah! That would be poor old Spencer Wells. I knew him well. I knew another of that jury too curiously enough. George Smith, Sandy Smith, of Smith, Robertson & Company. He died in Scotland some years ago. And what happened to the rest?"

"Well, sir, it seems that the man Box had a grudge against you all——"

"You should have seen his face when the foreman said the word 'guilty.' I never saw such hate on any face in my life before or since. And do you know, as the years have passed and I've grown older, and perhaps wiser,

I've had some terrible doubts as to the rightness of our verdict. Probably it's mostly sentiment, you know the sort of thing, condemning a fellow-creature to hew stones in Dartmoor for the rest of his life while we enjoy the country and flowers and things like that," he waved his hand in the direction of the green and summery landscape, "but apart from that, I've had qualms. There was something about the man's face—well, it's an old story and the man has been out for many years now. At least I hope he has. Is he still alive?"

"Very much so." Dewar was finding it difficult to explain the situation without giving Mr Field too great a shock. Nobody, however iron-nerved and brave, cares to hear suddenly that he is being pursued by a relentless and efficient murderer.

"Well, Inspector, what is it you want? The case isn't going to be re-opened after all these years like that fellow in Glasgow—what's his name—Slater?"

"No, sir. But the point is that Box had a grudge against you gentlemen who found him guilty. And we've every reason to suppose that as soon as he was released he set to work to work off his grudge."

Mr Field opened his eyes. "Did he indeed? And what form did his revenge take?"

"Ten of the jury are dead," said Dewar gravely, "and only two died peacefully at home and one was drowned."

Mr Field half-rose from his seat and stared at the Inspector with terrified eyes. His mouth had fallen open.

"Do you mean——" he began and Dewar spared him the trouble of framing the words.

"Yes, sir. That is what I mean. Harry Box has tracked the jurors down, one by one, and killed them in cold blood."

"My God," whimpered Mr Field. "What a ghastly thing! What a terrible thing! Are you sure, Inspector? Have you evidence for what you say? How can a Godalming policeman know all about this? I'll wait till I hear it confirmed from Scotland Yard."

"I am from Scotland Yard." Mr Field's mouth fell open again and he drummed nervously on the table with trembling fingers.

"My God," he said at last and could think of nothing else to say.

The Inspector judged that it would be best not to let him brood over his imminent danger and proceeded briskly.

"Now, Mr Field, if you will put yourself entirely in our hands I think we shall be able to see that you're not a penny the worse and that Master Box is laid by the heels."

"Of course, of course, I leave everything to you."

"Well then, sir, may I have a list of your household." Dewar pulled out a notebook.

"There is myself and my wife and an unmarried daughter."

"And your staff?"

"There is a butler and a chauffeur and a gardener and a knife-boy and—and—some maids. I'm not sure how many. There's a cook, of course, but my wife will tell you the rest."

"Very well, sir. Now, will you ask the three men to take a fortnight's holiday. I'll fill their places from headquarters."

"Excuse me a moment, my dear Inspector," cried Mr Field with gleaming eyes. "I have a much better plan. I will go at once upon a long sea-voyage, leaving you behind to secure this scoundrel."

"Won't do, sir, I'm afraid. It's ten to one the man would either lie low and wait for your return or else follow you."

"But you could arrest him while he was lying low."

"We might if we were lucky. But we might fail. We haven't the faintest idea where he is."

"Well, I call that most damnably incompetent," exclaimed Mr Field, his voice rising indignantly. "The man has committed a dozen murders."

"Not yet, sir," put in Dewar quietly and Mr Field collapsed like a balloon.

"I do think it's hard," he quavered, "for a man of my age to be used as a decoy for a desperate murderer. My nerves won't stand the strain. I know they won't."

"I can assure you, sir, that the full resources of Scotland Yard will be employed to defend you and that you will be as safe as it is humanly possible to make you."

"Very well, Sergeant, very well. I realise I have no alternative." Mr Field gazed at the detective with a woebegone haggardness that was very different from his confident manner on the lawn.

"Thank you, sir. Will you then send your men-servants away for a fortnight and allow me to use the telephone for a call to London?"

Mr Field nodded dazedly and stretched out a trembling hand for the bell. His butler entered. "Ah, Parkinson," began the master of the house nervously. "I want you to take a fortnight's holiday—on full pay, of course—and please tell George and Shaw and, and what the devil's the name of that boy——"

"William, sir."

"And William. They are all to take a fortnight's holiday."

"That is very kind of you, sir. I take it, sir, you are going away yourself?"

"No, no, no. I'm not going away."

"In that case, sir, I hardly see how you can spare us all at the same moment. For myself, sir, I do not require a holiday, thanking you very much all the same."

"Nonsense, Parkinson, I insist. I particularly want you all to go at once and not return for
a fortnight. You can have one of the cars to take you to the station."

The butler had read too many serial stories about impassive butlers to express the least surprise. He merely said, "Very good, sir. Do you wish us to go this week, sir?"

"Today, today. This afternoon."

The butler bowed and withdrew with a cold glance at Dewar who was busy with the telephone. Mr Field fell back in his chair and covered his face with his hands.

"Come, come, sir," said Dewar in a kindly tone. "It might have been much worse. You're in good hands. There are five of us here already and before the evening's out there'll be three more. You needn't worry. Besides, it's an even chance that he won't come here at all. My chief with another car-load of men has gone to the house of the other surviving juror," Mr Field shuddered, "in case he goes there first. In which case you won't be bothered."

"What shall I do? What shall I do?" whimpered Mr Field.

"Stay indoors and keep the shutters closed," answered Dewar briskly. "The man isn't
possessed of miraculous powers. All he's got is an air-pistol and amazing audacity. If you stay behind shutters he can't get you. Anyone coming near the house will be tackled by my men. We know roughly what he looks like and he won't stand a chance. There's absolutely nothing for you to worry about."

"Well, Sergeant, I hope you're right. I sincerely hope you're right. It is a terrible position for a man of my age to be put in. Twenty-five years ago and the murdering cut-throat has nursed his revenge all that time. It's terrible. Terrible."

While he was rambling on, Dewar was closing the shutters of the library. "I think it would be as well, sir," he said over his shoulder, "if you explained matters to your wife and arranged to have all your meals here. I don't want you to pass in front of unshuttered windows if you can help it."

"Indeed, indeed I won't. How would it be to shutter all the windows?"

"No, sir. I'm afraid that wouldn't do. Box would think either that you had gone away or that you had smelt a rat."

"Very well," sighed Mr Field.

"When you tell your wife, I want you to impress upon her the importance of not telling the maids. They must just think you've had a remarkable fit of eccentricity in sending your men-servants on a holiday and filling their places for a fortnight. If you mention police, the whole thing will be all over the village in an hour and our man will turn shy. They can guess what they like. It isn't probable that they'll guess the truth. If they do," he added grimly, "they ought to be at Scotland Yard."

Dewar proceeded to make a tour of the house, examining the doors, cellars, and windows through which entry was easy, and choosing posts of observation for his men. Then he walked round the garden, looking for the most probable lines of attack. The garden was perfectly suited for the methods of Harry Box. A lane at the back seemed to be even more deserted than that by which he had escaped after shooting Oliver Maddock. The wall was considerably lower than the wall of Greenlawns and there was a conveniently situated shrubbery. The more Dewar examined it the more certain he became that once again the attempt would be made from the garden rather than from the front of the house. After all, he reflected, Box had no reason to suspect that at last the police had got ahead of him. He had been so successful from the garden on two previous occasions that he would be almost certain to try it again. Dewar called up one of his men and asked him to climb a chestnut tree which grew just inside the wall and which overhung the lane. The plain-clothes man scrambled swiftly up the tree and was soon lost in the luxuriant foliage.

"Can you see the lane from there?" called up Dewar.

"Most of it, sir."

"You must find a place where you can see it all." There was a rustling and creaking of branches and then the detective called down, "All right, sir. I can see it all."

"Mark the place and come down then." The man scrambled down again. "Now," said Dewar, "go up to the village and buy half a dozen electric bells, batteries and a mile of wire. If you can't get them there, we'll have to send to Guildford. But you might try the village first. Then fit up a bell in the butler's pantry and a bell-push on that branch. Get the idea?"

"Yes, sir." The man went off and Dewar continued his tour. Two hours later a cordon of observation posts had been established round the house, each connected with an electric bell to the butler's pantry. The four slightly bewildered but decorously jubilant men-servants had left the house and Mr Field, seated in his shuttered library, was engaged in rallying his spirits with a fairly strong whisky and soda.

Inspector Dewar, like a spider at the centre of its web, sat in the pantry. The electric bells were neatly set out in a row on the table and beside him lay a revolver.

CHAPTER XXV

Out-Boxed

The long summer's day gradually faded into evening. Nothing happened in the neighbourhood of Witton House. The ring of watchers sat silent at their posts and there was no sound but the hum of a belated bee, the twitter of birds and the occasional hoot of a distant motor horn. At half-past six the Superintendent telephoned from Greytiles, the house of Mr John Young Boyd, to ask for news. There was none to give him. He approved of Dewar's system of vigilance and particularly praised the electric bells. "We may be here for weeks" were his last words. Night fell and the outer ring of sentinels was called in. The windows of the house were shuttered, the doors were carefully locked and bolted and detectives were posted on each floor.

At about two o'clock in the morning Dewar was awakened by a light touch on his shoulder. It was one of the sentries. "Man in the garden, sir," he replied.

Dewar sprang swiftly out of bed as if he had not been asleep a second before, threw on his overcoat and thrust his revolver into the pocket. "Lead on," he said briefly.

The detective tip-toed downstairs to the corner in a passage where he had been posted and pointed to the chink in the shutter which he had left open. Dewar peered through. It was a beautiful night of stars and a moon that was halfway to the full. The garden was full of shadows and silver dew. At first the Inspector could see nothing suspicious until suddenly one of the shadows moved and he could make out the dim silhouette of a man standing by one of the shrubberies.

Hardened and experienced though he was in crime of almost every description, Dewar could not prevent a shiver running down the small of his back. For months and months his mind had been occupied all day and every day with this mysterious, sinister and ruthless murderer. He had thought of nothing else. He had had only one object before him during all that time, and that object was to find himself face to face with the deadly killer. And there he was at last. Dark, shadowy, mysterious, he was planning his last crime. He was surveying the ground of his last deadly exploit. Dewar's mind flashed to the story he had read somewhere of Napoleon's landing on the coast of England to survey the ground for his invasion. In just such a way he might have stood, motionless in the half light of the moon, staring at the place he was going to attack.

Dewar wrenched his eyes from the chink with an effort. "Call the others," he whispered. "Two to come with me, two to go down the lane from the east and two to double across the field and join them from the west. Quick! I'll wait here."

The detective slipped upstairs to the bedrooms and Dewar put his eye again to the chink. The shadow was moving now, slowly, along the shrubbery on a line parallel with the house. Once it stopped for a moment and then went on again, never varying its leisurely pace. "Like a cat," muttered Dewar. "Like a confounded cat." He listened for the tip-toe footsteps of his men, wondering vaguely if bullets from an air-pistol hurt as much as real ones. The figure had stopped again in deeper shadow and was invisible for a moment or two. Dewar was beginning to wonder if the man had gone back into the bushes when it moved once more and at the same instant the sentry who had roused the inspector appeared at his elbow.

"All correct, sir," he whispered. "They've started."

Dewar nodded. Then he looked at his wrist watch.

"We'll give them three minutes to get into position. You stay here and look after the house. The other two follow me when I say 'go.'" He went to the back door and noiselessly slid the bolts and turned the key. "Ready?" he breathed over his shoulder and a double whisper answered him, "Yes, sir."

"Then come on." Dewar opened the door as quietly as he could and slipped out. The next moment he was tearing across the lawn with his two assistants at his heels. In front, he could hear the violent crackling of bushes and could see the branches of the shrubs waving agitatedly in the moonlight. Just as he reached the shrubbery a motor started in the lane and, by the time Dewar was astride the wall, had already moved thirty or forty yards. The inspector waited breathlessly. At any moment the motor would be halted by the two detectives who had made the detour in order to intercept the retreat, He fingered the trigger of his revolver anxiously and then, to his relief, came a loud shout of "Halt." The car, rapidly accelerating, drove on and vanished round a curve of the lane.

Dewar dropped from the wall and raced after it. At the curve he found one of his men lying unconscious on the road while the other was leaning against the wall with his arm across his forehead. The car had vanished.

"Sparkes, what is it? Are you hurt?" cried Dewar in an agony of apprehension lest the air-pistol had been at work again.

"Knocked on the head," muttered the detective in a dazed voice. "Ran slap into us." Dewar knelt over the other man and found to his relief that he was alive. He jumped up and gave hasty instructions to the two men who had followed him across the lawn to look after the injured men, and then he ran back to the house and telephoned to the Guildford police to look out for a single man in a four-seater car. All cars were to be stopped and the instruction passed to all neighbouring police stations.

By the time he had finished, the injured man had been brought in and examined. Constable Sparkes was able to explain what had happened. He and Constable James had arrived at the curve in the lane just as the car was under way. They had stood in the middle of the road and shouted "Halt." The car, which was being driven in one of the low gears, slowed up at once and they had therefore stood their ground. A yard distant the car had almost stopped and then the driver had put his foot hard on the accelerator. The car almost pounced on them like a wild animal and over they went. It was perfectly simple.

Dewar took up the telephone again and after a few minutes' delay was connected with Greytiles. The Superintendent was awake and Dewar told him what had happened. Bone was annoyed at the escape but blamed no one. "Of course your men couldn't have fired at him. I quite see that. But I don't see why you were in such a hurry to rush at him before you had him surrounded."

"It wasn't so easy to arrange to surround him at a moment's notice," protested Dewar, "and I was afraid of the air-pistol."

Bone was indignant. "Of course you were afraid of it. Who wouldn't be?"

"I mean I was afraid of someone else getting hit. It made me over-anxious to get at him myself."

There was a slight pause and then the Superintendent said, "You're a good fellow, Dewar. Good night," and rang off.

Shortly after eight o'clock that morning, Dewar was called to the telephone.

"A call from Reading," announced the operator. "Hold the line."

Dewar held the line. Then a voice said, "Is that the sergeant?"

"No," said Dewar. "It's not."

"This is Radford speaking, Constable Radford, sir. I'm speaking from Greytiles. Mr Boyd's place."

"This is Inspector Dewar speaking. Have you a message for me?"

"Yes, sir. We've got the man."

"What!" almost shouted Dewar. "You've got him?"

"Yes, sir. He must have come straight on here after leaving Witton. Anyway he ran straight into us."

"Is the Superintendent there? I would like to speak to him if he wouldn't mind," exclaimed Dewar eagerly.

"The Superintendent has gone into Reading, sir, with the prisoner. He asked me to telephone to you. He wants you to meet him in Reading as soon as you can with all your men."

"All of them? Are you sure?"

"That's my message, sir."

"Very well. Is that all?"

"Yes, sir."

Dewar rang off, shouted for one of his men and gave orders that the two cars should be got ready at once. Then he stared at the telephone. He was to leave Witton at once, with all his men. There was something odd about it. It was so sweeping, so exactly what Harry Box would like to happen, supposing that Harry Box was not in custody at Reading but was in a call office at, say, Godalming or Farnham.

He picked up the receiver and said, "I was called up just now. Can you tell me where the call came from?"

"Yes, sir," said the operator. "It was a Reading call."

"Thank you. Will you kindly get me Reading 0414.

There was a few minutes' wait and then a voice said, "Reading speaking. What number do you want?"

"0414," said Dewar. Again there was silence and then a different voice spoke.

"Hullo."

"Who am I speaking to?" asked Dewar. "This is Greytiles. Reading 0414."

"Is there a policeman there?"

"Yes. This is Constable Radford speaking. Who is that?"

"Oh, Radford, sorry to bother you. This is Dewar, Inspector Dewar. Would you mind repeating that message you gave me just now?"

"Certainly, sir. The Superintendent wants you to meet him with all your men at Reading as soon as you can, sir. The Superintendent has got the man you want."

"Thank you very much, Radford. Good-bye."

"Good-bye, sir."

Dewar went with a light heart and brisk step to the door of Mr Field's bedroom. Mr Field, pale and worn, opened the door and came out in his dressing gown.

"It's all over, sir," said the Inspector jovially. "We've got the man and he won't trouble you any more."

"You've got him?" cried Mr Field, clutching at his breast with his hand and leaning back, trembling, against the door post.

"We have, sir. He's under lock and key by this time."

Mr Field was paler than ever and shaking like a reed. "You'll excuse me. I must lie down. Good news is often as startling as bad," he tottered back into his bedroom and Dewar returned to his men.

The cars were ready and in five minutes the band of detectives were on their way to Reading. At Reading Dewar went straight into Avory's office and held out his hand. "Well, my lad," he said cheerily, "so we've done it at last."

"Done what?" said Avory blankly. "Got Harry Box, of course." Avory's face lit up. "No? Have you, by thunder. I'm glad to hear it."

"Hasn't Bone brought him here? He started an hour ago and more."

Avory shook his head. "Bone's not been here today."

"Hadn't you heard about Box?"

"Not a word."

"How very extraordinary! "Dewar looked at his watch. "Ten past nine. It was about five past eight that they rang up from Greytiles."

"Car breakdown," said Avory. "Must be. Sit down and have some breakfast. I'll send down to the canteen for some."

While eating his breakfast, Dewar recounted to Avory the events of the previous night at Witton, interrupting his narrative almost at the end by springing to his feet and exclaiming, "I say. Twenty-five to ten. An hour and forty minutes for six miles. We'd better telephone to Greytiles."

"Better than that would be to take a car and run out along the road. There's only one road and we can't miss them. We know they've left Greytiles."

Taking one plain-clothes man, the two Inspectors drove out in the direction of Mr John Young Boyd's house. They met no broken-down police car and it was not long before they found themselves at the entrance to the avenue of Greytiles.

"As we're here we'd better go in," said Dewar. "They must have turned back."

Half-way up the avenue a man sprang out from behind a tree, saluted smartly and vanished again. At the door another man was sitting on the steps. He jumped up and saluted.

"Morning, Brown," said Dewar. "Done a good morning's work, eh? Has the Superintendent gone up to London?"

"No, sir." As he spoke the Superintendent himself came to the door.

"Thought I recognised the accent of Dumbartonshire. Morning, Avory. Well, young man, what brings you here?"

"I waited in Reading, sir, and then I thought you must be broken down, so I came to look for you."

"That was kind of you. But what exactly was your idea?"

"Idea, sir? None."

"But, my good fellow, you must have some reason for leaving Witton and coming over here."

"Your message, sir."

"Message? What message?" Dewar suddenly went cold all over.

"Your telephone message. Radford rang me up and told me to meet you in Reading."

The Superintendent was standing like a statue. "Who's Radford?"

"One of your men, sir, I suppose."

"There's no one of that name here and I sent no message."

"My God," ejaculated Dewar in a whisper.

"If you've been taken in by a bogus telephone message, then it is a case of 'My God.'" The Superintendent spoke sternly. "And it will be the end of your career in the Force, James Dewar."

"But I wasn't taken in. I checked back."

"What!"

"Yes, sir. I waited five minutes and checked back."

"And what happened?"

"I got on to Greytiles and spoke to Radford and he gave me the identical message."

Bone never moved his eyes from Dewar's face. "Send Robbins here, Auger," he said. "What time did you get this message, Dewar?"

"Eight five."

"And you checked back at eight ten?"

"It would be nearer eight fifteen before I got through."

"Very good. Robbins."

"Sir."

"Were you on the telephone this morning?"

"Yes, sir."

"What hours?"

"From six onwards, sir."

"Did you have a call at eight-fifteen?"

"There was no call between six and nine twenty-two, sir."

"Nothing from Inspector Dewar?"

"No, sir."

"What number did you call, Dewar?"

"Reading 0414, sir."

"What is the number of this house, Robbins?"

"Reading 0414, sir."

"It is the only instrument in the house?"

"Yes, sir."

"Very well. That's all, Robbins. As for you, Dewar, you'd better get back to Witton at once. I'll come with you. Avory, will you take charge here and carry on. Telephone to Reading and send back Dewar's men to Witton as fast as they can go. And telephone to Witton and warn Mr Field. Though it's a fiver to a farthing that the man's dead by now. Come on, Dewar."

CHAPTER XXVI

Number Eleven

Anyone taking Superintendent Bone's odds of a fiver to a farthing against Mr Field being still alive at half-past ten that morning would have lost a farthing. The Superintendent and the Inspector arrived at Witton after a headlong drive across country to find confusion, fear and mourning at Witton House. Mr Field had been shot while seated at breakfast by a man who had suddenly appeared at the dining room window. Mrs Field was sitting at the time with her back to the window, reading an illustrated daily paper. A shadow fell across her paper and a voice said, "You sent me to twenty-five years in hell, Field. I'm sending you to eternity in hell." Mrs Field jumped up and turned round to the window. A man was looking in and he held a pistol. There was the sound of a gentle sneeze followed by a crash as Mr Field fell, face downwards amid the breakfast cups. The assassin flicked a piece of cardboard on to the table and then Mrs Field fainted. That was all that was known. The murder took place at about a quarter to nine or perhaps a few minutes later.

Bone was very grim as he listened to the story, fingering the square of white cardboard on which was written the word "Eleven."

At the end he said, "There's nothing to do here except go to the post office."

In silence the two men drove to the village post office. A small knot of people was standing in the road outside it, staring at the door.

"What's up?" asked Bone as he got out of the car.

"Post office shut, sir," answered one of the loiterers civilly. "Open at eight and 'tis now half-past eleven. Miss Baines must be ill."

"Lives alone there, eh?" said Bone.

"Yes, sir. Lives over the office."

"Come on, Dewar," said the Superintendent. "We must break it open."

The two detectives at once began a scientific attack on the door, to the surprise and admiration of the group of villagers, and in a few moments had broken the lock and entered. On the threshold Bone turned and addressed the now excited onlookers. "Please don't come in. We are police officers. Will one of you bring the village policeman?" A reluctant youth, after some hesitation, set off at a slow trot down the street while the remainder stood as near to the door as they dared.

Bone closed the door behind them and at once they became aware of a low moaning sound, proceeding from an inner room. The intervening door was also locked but only held out for a second or two and the detectives pushed into the room. On a sofa lay a large shapeless mass of light brown sacking which moved spasmodically and from which emanated the occasional moans.

Dewar whipped out a pocket knife. "Yes," murmured Bone. "Undo her. Miss Baines in her own parcel bags."

In a very short time the unfortunate postmistress was released and as soon as the gag had been removed from her mouth she instantly began to make up for the hours of enforced silence. Briefly, her story was as follows. She opened the office as usual at eight o'clock. Two minutes later a man came in and asked for a telegraph form. She came round the little counter with a new pad of forms, was seized, tied hand and foot, gagged and thrust into the large letter bags, and deposited on the sofa, all in about thirty seconds. At any rate it seemed about thirty seconds to her. From the inner room she could faintly hear voices speaking off and on for several minutes, then the sound of doors being locked and then silence until the entry of the detectives.

By the time the voluble and indignant lady had completed her narrative, the village constable had arrived. Bone rapidly introduced himself, handed over the situation and returned to the car. For half an hour he did not speak. Dewar was too unhappy to venture to say anything. At last Bone said, "I don't see how you can be blamed, Dewar. It was really most extraordinarily ingenious. No wonder you thought it was all right when you checked back. I'd have been taken in myself."

Dewar felt a load roll off his mind. Bone's words meant that there would not be an adverse report and that his career was not at an end.

"Thank you, sir," was all he could trust himself to say.

"But mind you," went on Bone warningly. "We've got to lay this man by the heels pretty soon or there'll be trouble for both of us. There isn't the shadow of an excuse now. We've got his name, his exact description, his motive, everything. It can't be more than a matter of hours. It mustn't be more than a matter of hours." Dewar, who was driving, nodded and they went in silence for ten minutes until Bone broke out abruptly, "This is the worst case I've ever handled. I've never known a case in which everything went so completely wrong from start to finish. The only thing to be said in our favour is that, so far as I know, the motive is absolutely unique in the annals of crime. I can't recall another. Men have killed judges out of revenge, particularly in America, and even prosecuting counsel. But the jury! Never to my knowledge."

"The man's mad, of course."

"Yes. I think he is. Just mad enough to have this obsession and not mad enough to give himself away. The simplicity of the murders is a sign of madness and the way in which he vanishes in between them. Where does he go to, Dewar? Where does he vanish to? Somebody must see him, you'd think. And his description's been all over the place. Probably his madness makes him hide in the Regent Palace Hotel or the Carlton or somewhere where everyone can see him."

Bone relapsed into indignant silence and did not speak again until the car drew up at Greytiles.

Avory came out to meet them.

"No news is there, Avory?" called out Bone and Dewar thought that he could detect a note of apprehension in his voice.

"No, sir. Quiet as a mouse," returned the Reading inspector cheerfully.

Bone sat in the car for a full minute after it stopped and then jumped out briskly. "Come, then. We must have a conference. Is Mr Boyd about the place?"

"In his study."

Mr Boyd was an elderly man with white hair, a rosy complexion and clear brown eyes. He had a courteous and dignified manner and he rose from his chair to welcome his three visitors.

"Ah! my gallant defenders," he said, "Come in. You are welcome. I feel like Priam at the siege of Troy, seated in the safest part of the palace while the young men go out to fight his battles. Sit down."

"Mr Boyd," began the Superintendent gravely. "You are the last surviving member of the jury which found Harry Box guilty."

Mr Boyd looked keenly at him. "You mean that Mr Field——"

"This morning. At about nine o'clock." Mr Boyd's steady eyes never flinched. "Then I may expect an unwelcome visitor at any moment now."

"Yes. I want to tell you, if I may, what I have been thinking about it."

"I should be glad if you would, Superintendent. It is a matter which is of some interest to me." Mr Boyd gallantly forced a smile.

"The position, as I see it, is this," proceeded Bone. "There are two courses. The first is that you stay here, keeping behind shutters, strongly guarded by a select force of detectives under Inspector Dewar, while we scour England for Box. That course has this drawback. Although personally I think it is only a matter of hours before we catch him, we mustn't deny the possibility of failure. The man's mad and madmen are awkward people. It might conceivably be weeks or even months before we run him down. Now that he knows you are guarded, he is certain to lie low for a long time before making an attack on you and, of course, that will make it all the harder for us. You follow me, sir?"

"Perfectly."

"The alternative is for you to go abroad, preferably on a long sea-voyage to some destination that only you and I know. You would close this house, send away your furniture and put the house in the hands of agents to sell for you, and let it be known that you are leaving the neighbourhood under doctor's orders and never returning. Sooner or later Box will hear that you've gone. To everyone else your sudden departure from a neighbourhood in which you've lived all your life will seem amazing and inexplicable. To Box alone it will seem perfectly natural. It will be a panic-stricken flight. You no longer trust the law and the police to protect you. You want to put ten thousand miles between you and the avenger. Then what will happen? Box will sooner or later come to make enquiries to find out where you're gone. He won't dare to come too soon for fear of running into a trap, but he won't dare to leave it too late for fear of the scent going cold. If we haven't caught him in a month or so, then he'll come creeping back to get on to your trail. Of that I'm positive. It's become an obsession with him to avenge himself on the jurymen and he's so close to the completion of the job that he'll risk anything to bring it off. That's how I see it."

Bone lay back in his chair and mopped his brow. So much talking made him hot.

"You put the case very clearly and frankly," said Mr Boyd. "Do I have to make up my mind at once?"

"Oh no. But it would be a great help if you could decide today."

"And which do you advise?"

"I advise you to go away."

"May I give you my answer in half an hour? I shall be able to come to a definite decision by then."

"Certainly, sir."

"Then perhaps you will be kind enough to return in half an hour."

At the end of the prescribed half-hour, the three detectives once more entered the shuttered library.

"Gentlemen," said Mr Boyd as they came in, "I have made up my mind. I will go abroad. I can't stand the prospect of spending months behind these shutters."

"I think you are wise, sir," answered Bone. "I will go up to London at once and make all arrangements for your departure. Is there anyone who you think would care to accompany you?"

"I have a niece who would come, I am sure. She is fond of travel and gets very little opportunity of indulging in her fondness."

"Then if you will give me her address I will arrange it. In the meantime, perhaps you will be kind enough to give instructions for a trunk or two to be packed. You will be leaving some time tomorrow morning."

Next morning the inhabitants of the surrounding district were astonished to learn from their local newspaper that Mr John Young Boyd, one of the best known and most respected citizens in the district, had suddenly left his house at Greytiles and, acting on urgent medical advice, had gone away to take up his residence abroad. Greytiles and its contents were to be placed very shortly on the market. Friends who walked, rode or drove over to the house on that very morning were still more astonished to find that Mr Boyd had already gone without a word of farewell. Notice boards from various house agents had already begun to sprout over the front wall like quick-growing funguses. The familiar housemaid had already been replaced by a solemn, heavily-built caretaker and an omnibus was standing at the door for the removal of the belongings of the domestic staff.

Tradesmen with outstanding accounts came tearing up to the back door and were delighted to find that the caretaker had been authorised to pay all bills. The local doctor, who had been under the impression that Mr Boyd was mentally and physically as sound as a bell, was as taken aback as anyone, but naturally he did not say so. He shook his head and announced that there was more in it than met the eye.

So the trap was set.

CHAPTER XXVII

The Trap is Set

For three weeks nothing happened. The nine-days' wonder of Mr Boyd's departure was not displaced by any sensational incident from being the chief topic of conversation in the vicinity. A number of clients came from the house agents with "orders to view" Greytiles but were unanimous in declaring, loudly, so that the stolid caretaker could hear, that the price asked was utterly fantastic and that no one in their senses would give half of it. The search for Harry Box was carried on with unrelenting vigour all over the country and reports poured into Superintendent Bone's office at Scotland Yard of suspicious characters, of important information, of arrests that had been made or were about to be made. But every alarm was a false alarm. Of Harry Box and his motor car there was no sign. Meanwhile Inspector Dewar and half a dozen picked men walked, bicycled and loitered day after day in the road, lanes, woods and fields round Greytiles. Every evening, after nightfall, the inspector slipped quietly into the house by the back entrance to hear the report of the caretaker on the happenings of the day. It was more than likely that Box would come to see the house with an 'order to view' on the chance of picking up some useful information and the man who had been selected for the post of caretaker was one of the three Scotland Yard experts in make-up and disguise.

An outer cordon of plain-clothes men bicycled tirelessly from garage to garage in a circle of about five miles' radius round Greytiles. All reports were telephoned to the caretaker who passed them on to Dewar in the evenings.

After three weeks of ceaseless but monotonous vigil Dewar received a pencil note from Bone, which ran as follows: "Dear D. Expect you're getting pretty fed up. Don't forget that if our idea is right H. B. should be appearing soon. Yours, J. B., Supt."

Dewar passed on the message to his subordinates and the patrolling was carried out with increased zest and vigilance. On the night after Bone's letter arrived, the caretaker reported an unusual incident. It was part of his duty to put all Mr Boyd's letters into a large envelope and forward them to the Superintendent who in turn sent them on to Mr Boyd. It was also part of his duty, though Mr Boyd was unaware of this, to steam open all the envelopes, read the letters and shut them again in case there might be any threatening or warning letters. On the day in question two envelopes had contained blank sheets of paper. He had tried the ordinary tests for invisible ink and had obtained no results. Dewar took the letters and envelopes and sent a man up to London with them by the last express from Reading. Next morning Scotland Yard telephoned that the letters contained no invisible ink and the sheets of paper were perfectly blank. That morning there were two more letters containing blank sheets and these were duly forwarded to London with the same result. There was no invisible writing on them. On the following day there were three letters, and then came a halt in the mysterious correspondence for three days. Dewar felt uneasy but he could not explain why. He was a matter-of-fact, straightforward man who was quite prepared to arrest a murderer or stop a runaway horse or rescue people from a burning house, all in the day's work. He was not in the least afraid of straightforward situations, of people, things and incidents that he could see and understand. But the idea of this invisible, maniacal murderer had begun to appal him. It was nearly a month since he had started his vigil at Greytiles and nothing had happened except the arrival by post of a few bits of blank paper. Those blank sheets worried him. He felt that they were part of some weird, subtle, unheard of manoeuvre, the sort of thing that could only emanate from the brain of a madman and the sort of thing that an ordinary, sane inspector of police would be unable to comprehend and combat. His matter-of-fact common sense assured him that a few bits of blank paper could do no one any harm; his subconscious imagination instinctively drew pictures of some prodigious and fantastic villainy in which those papers played a big part. Somehow they seemed like the first breach in the walls, the first shots fired by the silent and invisible enemy in the last battle of this long-drawn and merciless campaign. It took a lot to rattle Inspector Dewar but that dour Scotsman confessed to himself that he was nearer to being rattled than he had been since his days as a raw uniformed policeman.

When the blank sheets began to appear again, after an interval of three days, Dewar rang up the Superintendent and asked for advice. Bone simply said, "You must give me time to think. Ring up in an hour," and rang off.

In an hour Dewar tried again. This time Bone was not so laconic. "I've got an idea about those letters," he said. "It's the result of some hard thinking and I give it to you for what it's worth. Can you hear me?"

"perfectly, sir."

"Very well, then. What about this? Our friend H.B. thinks that our other friend J.Y.B. has beat it out of sheer funk and left a caretaker to forward letters. He wants to know where those letters are going, so he decides to intercept the outgoing mails. But it's not a trick that he'll be able to play twice, so he's got to make certain that there are mails on the day and at the hour that he's going to intercept. So he posts the letters himself."

"But why every day?"

"To get the caretaker accustomed to the idea of posting letters and also in case no address was left at first. On getting the first letter, the caretaker might have to write or telegraph for an address. Therefore H.B. has to give him time. That's my contribution to your worries. You can make what you like of it."

Dewar considered this theory and the more he considered it the more he liked it. With his native frankness he admitted to himself that he liked it, not so much for its probable correctness, but because it provided a perfectly sane and ordinary solution of an incident which he was beginning to invest with a diabolical or supernatural subtlety. The blank letters, instead of being some incredible device of a maniacal genius, would become simply the trick of an ordinarily clever man. At any rate, whether the theory was right or wrong, Dewar determined to act upon it. A word with Avory, passed on by him to the Reading postmaster, quickly assured the replacement of the Greytiles postman by a plain clothes detective in postman's uniform, and Dewar arranged to spend the night in the back room of the Greytiles post office, sharing watch duty with the driver of the police car. He also moved the police car from its garage in the village to a shed a few yards distant from the post office.

The flow of blank letters continued spasmodically. On some days there were five or six, on other days not more than one. They were addressed in varying handwritings, posted from different parts of London in different shapes, sizes and qualities of envelope. Every day they were carefully re-addressed by the caretaker to a fictitious address in the Irish Free State and handed to the new postman.

The search for Harry Box was beginning to flag. Newspapers which had offered large rewards for information leading to his arrest, doubled the rewards and then forgot all about them as new topics submerged the series of murders in public interest. The posters containing his photograph and description began to be defaced by time and weather and were not reposted. The police search continued unabated but the public did not know that. In the absence of newspaper headlines, the public assumed that the case was practically dropped and that the most detestable and hideous series of murders since the days of Jack the Ripper had passed into the all-too-long list of undiscovered crimes.

This view was confirmed in a short but weighty leading article in *The Times* which caused a brief flare-up of interest for a couple of days and then journalistic silence descended once more on the murders of the Reading jurymen.

It was exactly five weeks after the departure of Mr John Young Boyd for an unknown destination that the murderer made his last appearance.

CHAPTER XXVIII

Beloved Wife of H.B.

It was at about three o'clock in the morning, in the middle of one of Dewar's turns as sentry, that there came the faint sound of metal scraping on metal at the front door of the Greytiles Post Office. Dewar, who had been sitting in an easy chair, utterly bored and weary of his long weeks of inaction, sat up in the darkness and listened. There was silence for ten or fifteen seconds and then the gentle scrape again. This time it was followed by a slight creak, as if someone was pushing against the door. Dewar softly awoke his assistant and was relieved that the man was sufficiently well trained to wake without a sound. While the policeman chauffeur was hastily slipping on his boots, Dewar knelt at the slightly opened door which led into the public room of the post office and peered through the chink. Everything was in darkness. The shutters of the office were up and not even the faintest gleam of moonlight penetrated them. The scraping stopped again and a loud click resounded startlingly loud throughout the room. The lock of the door had been turned from the outside. There was another slight creak and a rustle and Dewar could see a long strip of faint light which grew wider and wider until at the top of it he could make out a star and below it the outline of a tree against the sky. Both were blacked out the next instant by a dark shadow which slipped into the room without a sound. Then they re-appeared and were blacked out again by the swift closing of the door. Harry Box was in the post office.

Dewar quickly backed on his knees from the chink and he was not a moment too soon. A thin ray of light whirled round the outer room, came to rest on the chink and then went out. The two detectives remained kneeling on the floor in the dark, holding their breaths. Dewar had drawn his pistol but did not dare to cock it. The click would have sounded almost as loud as a shot in that close space and deep silence. He made up his mind that if the light came round the door he would have to do his best to cock his pistol and fire simultaneously. There was no use risking that deadly air-pistol at close quarters. In a rush across a garden it was bad enough. But in a village post office it was simple suicide.

Dewar held his breath till his temples began to drum and just as he felt that his next breath was bound to be almost a heavy sigh and might well be his last, the door between the two rooms closed with an unmistakable snap and a bolt slipped into place.

The inspector sprang to his feet in a flash, thrust his pistol into his pocket and tip-toed to the window. Very slowly, inch by inch, he raised it until there was room to wriggle through. Once outside, he waited for his assistant to follow him and then he ventured on a whisper, "Can you see me?"

"Yes," whispered the other. "Then follow."

He led the way round the post office towards the road, halting for a second when he was halfway round to cock his automatic and mutter in the chauffeur's ear, "We'll get him as he comes out." They crept stealthily forward to the front of the building and took post one on each side of the door by which the stranger had entered, crouching like two tigers ready for the deadly pounce. Dewar risked a single swift look through the keyhole but could see nothing except the reflection of a dim light. For several minutes they waited, tense and grim in the shadows, their eyes riveted to the handle of the door, which they could just distinguish in the darkness. At last it began to turn, very slowly. Dewar braced himself for the supreme effort and he could hear his subordinate draw a quick breath. And then a fierce barking broke out behind them. The handle slipped promptly back into its place and an indignant terrier, returning from some nocturnal expedition, hurled itself in an ecstasy of fury and rage and noise at the two crouching detectives. The fearless animal did his best to bite them both simultaneously and was greatly encouraged by their complete impassivity. Neither of them moved a muscle under the unexpected and disastrous intervention. A neighbouring dog came charging out of its kennel to the full length of a rattling chain and joined in the noise and in less than half a minute a dozen dogs were in full blast, led by the infuriated terrier.

Under cover of the din, the Inspector managed to whisper, "Don't move." It required all his concentration to keep his eyes fixed upon the handle and not to glance at the menacing dog who was by now firmly convinced that strangers who crouch in doorways at three o'clock in the morning are up to no good and was redoubling his efforts. Dewar cursed his luck. Luck had gone against him from the very start of the whole business and now when he had his hand on the murderer, after all these months, luck turned up again in the form of a little brute of a barking dog. It was all Dewar could do to restrain himself from shooting it on the spot, or, alternatively, from shooting down the lock of the door and making a final desperate attack on Box. Suddenly the terrier stopped barking as abruptly as he had begun. The Inspector with a great effort of will kept his eyes on the handle, but when he heard a single yelp and the pattering of paws on the road, he could not help throwing a glance over his shoulder. Instantly he realised that the dog had changed sides. A dark figure was tearing down the road towards Reading with the terrier in full pursuit. Dewar sprang up with an exclamation of "The back window," thrust his pistol into his pocket and rushed after the fugitive, his subordinate at his heels. The quarry had gained almost a hundred yards' start by slipping behind a group of outhouses and barns before rejoining the road, and Dewar, whose brain was racing as fast as his feet, jerked an order over his shoulder, "Go back for the car," and, ran on alone. In ten seconds the wisdom of his tactics was proved for a couple of white lights and a red light sprang into being down the road. A motor car was standing in the dark shadows of a line of trees. An instant later the engine started and Dewar fumbled in his pocket for his pistol. He was within fifty yards of the car when it began to move and he steadied himself for a shot. Just as he slipped the safety-catch down he stumbled over the returning terrier and fell headlong in the road. The automatic went off with a deafening clap and a small branch of a tree fluttered slowly to the ground. By the time Dewar had sprung to his feet the car was in third gear and travelling well. A pistol shot was out of the question. Dewar turned and gazed into the darkness towards Greytiles. The flash of the shot had dazzled him into temporary blindness and he could see nothing. He stood motionless, counting aloud slowly. At fifteen he was wondering what the Commissioner would say; at twenty he could almost hear the laughter at the Yard when it came out that a terrier dog had prevented him from arresting a murderer; at twenty-five he was feeling bitterly that Box's air-pistol was preferable to being sacked from the Force and at thirty the headlights of the police car swung slowly out of the shed on to the Reading road. Box had just over half a minute's start, he reflected, as he jumped on to the running board and clambered in beside the driver, and Police Constable Harrison was the finest driver at headquarters.

It was an even chance.

At first the pursuit was comparatively simple. The fugitive kept his headlights on and their glare was visible for a long distance. Nor was there much danger of confusing them with the headlights of other cars at that hour of the morning. The big police car fell behind at first, the engine being cold, but gradually it warmed up and the pace increased. Police Constable Harrison sat like an amiable Sphinx at the wheel, driving with an ease and brilliance that Dewar envied. The car in front turned and twisted in a maze of small country lanes between Beech Hill and Aldermaston, and once the pursuers lost valuable seconds in running past a cross-roads and having to back. Fortunately when they were on the right road again they could just make out the beams of the headlights in front. But after a quarter of an hour's wild chase the dawn began to break behind them and Box switched off his headlights as he ran through Aldermaston.

"That's done it," muttered Dewar and the driver spoke for the first time. "If we go right it takes us on to the Bath Road; left is to Kingsclere and Andover. Straight on are more lanes." Box's car had vanished but an early riser in Aldermaston directed them towards the Bath Road. A valuable twenty seconds was lost in making the enquiry.

"Left to Newbury, right to Reading and London," observed Harrison as they neared the Bath Road.

"Newbury?" said Dewar. "Newbury? We'll make it Newbury."

Once on the main road the powerful car had an opportunity of making up what had been lost in the country lanes, and between Thatcham and Newbury they caught a glimpse of a fast moving car ahead. Harrison for the first time leant forward slightly over his wheel and the pace increased a little.

"Seventy-one," said Dewar.

"Speedometer's wrong, sir. Not more than sixty-nine."

They crashed into the outskirts of Newbury at forty miles an hour and swept into the main street. A policeman who had been standing in the middle of the road with his back to them sprang at the pavement like a rabbit and shouted at them.

"Drive on," said Dewar. "He passed this way."

It was now almost daylight, the half-light between night and day, and as the police car reached the end of the town the detectives could see a four-seater car with a single occupant going fast up the hill on the Winchester road.

Police Constable Harrison leant back again and put the police car hard at the hill, while Dewar glanced at his pistol.

The man in front looked round for the first time but Dewar was not near enough to see his face. Another minute passed and the man looked round again. Dewar could see his high cheek-bones and sunken cheeks. The detectives were gaining rapidly and not more than fifty yards separated the two cars. A few more seconds and they would be up to him.

Then Harry Box had his last stroke of luck. As he passed a farm the first of a herd of cows ambled out of the gate on its way to pasture and halted behind him in the middle of the road. Harrison jammed on his four-wheel brakes, swerved almost into the ditch, skidded a dozen yards and brought his car back on to the top of the road past the cow. The whole manoeuvre lasted perhaps one second, but the loss of speed was enough to let Harry Box gain a hundred yards and vanish round a corner. The police car was after him in a flash and in twenty seconds Harrison was again jamming on his brakes. A car was standing at the lych-gate of Newtown Church and a man was running hard down the path to the church. Dewar sprang out of the police car and tore after him, pistol in hand. As he reached the church there came in the still morning air the sound of a suppressed sneeze and he instinctively ducked. Then he ran on and found himself alone in the churchyard. There was no one else there. He looked round and his eye caught a dark form lying across one of the graves. He ran across and turned it over. It was the body of a tall, dark man, with high cheekbones and sunken cheeks. A pistol of unusual pattern was clutched in his right hand and there was a small wound in his forehead.

Inspector Dewar looked at the tombstone of the grave. On it was written: "Here lies Mary, daughter of John Carpenter. Born October 4th, 1880. Died January 13th, 1921." And underneath had been scratched in crude lettering: "Beloved wife of H.B."